CRACKS and Other Short Stories

AFRICA TALENT PUBLISHERS [PVT] LTD
... home to Africa's finest talent

Masvingo, Zimbabwe

Albert Munyoro

Africa Talent Publishers

15155

Runyararo West

Masvingo, Zimbabwe

Email: mmawere@atpublishers.co.zw

tmubaya@atpublishers.co.zw

Tel: +263 776 966 915/+263 772 973 019

Website: http://www.atpublishers.co.zw/

ISBN: 9781779295408

© *Albert Munyoro*, 2019

About the Author

Albert Munyoro was born in 1968 in Gutu, Gonye village, under Chief Munyaradzi. He attended Mutero CPS and Guzha for his primary education and Mutero and Dadaya High Schools for his O-Level and A-Level, respectively. As a student, he was twice a national winner in the NRB sponsored secondary school essay competitions. He co-authored **Changed Lives: Testimonies from Zimbabwe** in 1995. In 2003 and 2006, he wrote short stories for Masvingo province's two leading weekly newspapers: *Masvingo Star* and *Mirror*. He wrote his second Christian book **Rapture Knocks** in 2018, **Cracks and other short stories** is his latest literary work. He taught at schools which include Chingele, Rafomoyo and Mutero High. Currently, he teaches English Language and A-Level Literature in English at Rufaro High School. He holds a C.E. (Secondary) and a BA with Education degree from Hillside Teachers College and Africa University, respectively. He is married and is a pastor-cum-teacher.

TABLE OF CONTENTS

DEDICATION

To all people who were or are candles in my
life, especially the Tagutanazvo, Kufa,
Mavedzenge families and my mother, Esther
Masiya, who bore burdens that some men
cannot bear.

ACKNOWLEDGEMENTS

I am deeply indebted to a number of people and institutions for their varying contributions towards the production of this anthology.

- Mr Zengeya, now late, who when I was in Grade 5 at Mutero CPS and read my English Creative work to the class and told me how wonderfully well I had written it, sowing the first seeds of my love for writing.
- Phillip Mavedzenge, my uncle, for encouragement in writing and the editors of *Masvingo Star* and *Mirror Newspapers* who watered the creative seed in me by publishing my stories.
- My colleagues at Mutero High School between the years 1998-2005 who relished reading my short stories and encouraged me to have them published for public consumption. These include Mr Kandororo, Mr Mmethie and Miss O. Zidenga.
- My Africa University lecturer, Mr John Crowe, for doubting my story on "Cracks" was original until he realised

there was a rare inherent creative talent in me.

- Africa Talent Publishers for believing my work was worth reading and hence, published it for public consumption. Thank you for offering me this rare opportunity.
- My wife, Loveness Munyoro and my children for moral support.
- Virginia Ndlovu for typing meticulously.

INTRODUCTION

CRACKS and OTHER SHORT STORIES is a collection of short stories, the majority which appeared in *Masvingo Star Newspaper* and a few in *Mirror Newspaper* in 2003 and 2006. They have, however, metamorphosed and appear in this anthology with slight changes in titles and even content after continuous working and reworking.

All the stories herein contained rest on the premise that most, if not all of our social, religious, political and cultural systems are characterised by metaphorical cracks that threaten their functions and existence and hence, endanger humanity in the process. In this regard, these widening cracks take on marital, religious, educational, cultural and political dimensions. To that end, the current production is reminiscent of Chinua Achebe's *No Longer At Ease* and *Things Fall Apart* as everything appears to be in a state of disequilibrium.

This anthology is unique in a number of ways. First, while the author has exercised his creative prowess and imagination, a number of events alluded to are historical truths. To exemplify, the reference to the state of Gutu-Mupandawana Bus terminus, the deaths of comrades on specified farms in Majumba Farming area in Chivhu, transport blues on our roads and the unending bank queues and the struggles to get money, are historical truths. In other words, some of the stories do not deal with the author's exclusive creative genius and imaginative precocity, but a life that was experienced and tasted by Zimbabweans. It can't be therefore, far from the truth to say some of the stories are historical stories fused with creative and imaginative ingenuity.

Second, most of the stories have a very profound rural flavour. The author displays an unparalleled nostalgia for the richness and beauty of undiluted rural life. He bemoans a lost culture and identity and yearns to re-live the simple and holistic rural life of the early 1970s going backwards. It is a life he identified with as a teenager. This era is characterised by sublime innocence in his view as adolescence of both sexes intermingled in childhood games and plays without any reports of sexual misconducts reported to adults unlike the current trends where our youths often experiment with sex without reservations.

Third, in this anthology, the teacher has been accorded modest eminence by being offered the greatest space and is celebrated unreservedly and prodigiously, so to speak. Put it in other words, the teacher is presented as a proverbial "candle" which burns itself out so that others can revel in their brightness. To say the least, in our contemporary society, the position of the teacher has been greatly compromised, demonised and cheapened. Gone are the days when learners aspired to be teachers when they grow up. Teaching has become the last desperate resort for our children but ironically everyone expects these demotivated and despised professionals to produce quality learners! The economic woes the teacher has been victim to, have undressed him/her and has all the remaining pockets of dignity deeply eroded. The behaviour of the teacher in the unending bank queues in *Caught Up In Battle* and the deplorable rutted attire of Mr Tsuro in *The Hands We Passed Through* is heart –rending and uncharacteristic of the teachers of yester-years. The plight of the resigned teachers as they wait for "decades" to have their retirement packages processed as if the processing is done by alien bureaucratic systems in faraway lands, is regrettable and needs due attention of the powers that be. That the teachers should languish in abject poverty when most of those who pass through their hands and those without a profession, lead better lives is not only sad to hear but very unfortunate. The voice of the passing wind at the end of *The Hands We Passed Through* is noteworthy here: Only in Germany are teachers paid handsomely and their roles and duties rewarded and celebrated.

Even worse to realise in Zimbabwe is that, the whole education system is under spotlight as schools continue to churn out learners with chains of distinctions that lead them nowhere except to disappointments and shattered hopes as many of them remain unemployed and surrender into destitution after school. Is the curriculum still relevant as was in the yester-years? That is the enduring question that lingers with echoes of despair. The updated curriculum implemented later in 2017 is indeed an attempt at mending metaphorical educational cracks. The message is clear: Give the teachers their rightful position in society, pay them well so that they cease to be cheap beggars who are society's laughingstocks and rugs; restore their dignity and self-esteem so that they can discharge their duties with confidence, motivation and dignity.

On this note, this work is a critical interrogation of a number of issues. While lamenting, it interrogates the accelerated cultural erosion especially in *Before I Die* and *Emptiness*. Equally, religious fanatism and hypocrisy is lambasted in *Time Bomb*. Also, the lack of responsibility by care-givers is exposed and mercilessly interrogated in many stories especially in *When the Maid Strikes, Emptiness, Twice a Mother The Unfair Penalty, Time Bomb* and *The Consequences* where the innocent suffers as a consequence of others' recklessness and meanness.

The land issue is central to the Zimbabwean people and the issue of land invasions and the role of the Svosve people as well as the reactions of European commercial farmers to the "land-grabbers" actions is treated with remarkable emotion. Even here, there are inherent cracks that need mending to redress land imbalances.

The list is endless: corruption, bureaucracy and infidelity in marriages are not spared either but the author's tone remain conciliatory and advisory. Let us mend all the cracks wherever they are and create a more conducive atmosphere where everyone can be relatively happy, peaceful and self-satisfied.

The behaviour of "hwindis" – the so-called rank marshals, the touts, leaves one appalled; they are the proverbial beasts that munch away at the livelihood of their own kind. Everyone sane fears them for they have the hearts of stones. They assault, threaten and hurl abusive words at their elders who by virtue of their ages deserve respect and honour. The police, it is apparent, have a resigned attitude and just look on as innocent people are victimised by callous touts. Has the love of money overtaken the youths to such extents? And the reasons the elderly and everyone is stripped of their monies? To get money for scuds at the wretched asbestos beer outlet on the bus terminus! The question of *Ubuntu/Unhu* therefore comes into focus.

Then last but not least, the ravaging effects of HIV and Aids in a world void of ARVs are graphically portrayed. Contracting HIV and Aids in the era under question spelled doom to the victims and society at large as the youths who should bury their elders are the once being buried by their elders. It's like tables turned upside down. The mental and emotional traumas of Aids victims are presented in a touching manner. The need to empathise and have supporting networks for the patients is underscored with the profundity and dexterity it deserves.

Our present society has ever widening cracks! So much has gone and is still going wrong not until conscientised individuals or groups and organisations stand up determinedly to correct what has gone amiss, where the whole house is falling apart. There is indeed hope to create better societies for our people. It all starts by being empowered to know what has gone wrong and how it all started and how we can strategically plan to mend the cracks.

*****

CRACKS

She just sat there glued to the same hot spot; the edge of a crudely home-made wooden bed, the product of cheap untrained village carpenters zealous to earn a few easy dollars with which to buy a few mugful of opaque beer at daily village beer parties. On her now aching lap, the crumbled ailing heap still lay, motionless like a log, midst the womb of the gross blackness of the summer night that buried them. Sleep evaded her that wretched night for they say sleep comes with peace of mind. One morning, but she was still wide awake like a witch; only little Ropafadzo snored soundly smiling in her sleep, silently mocking her. To be young! To be old too!

She consoled herself that it was the beginning of a new thing for, under the sky, many novel things begin and of course, end. The catechist at the mission school had said it well thirty years ago – thirty glorious years ago – when to be young was to be the king, was to possess all the joy and peace the world could offer, was to be genuinely innocent and carefree. It was playing and playing into the

1

night especially on moony nights. Play was the children's work. The second youthful preoccupation was gorging food. It was incessant feeding; there were wild fruits like *matamba, nhunguru, tsvanzva* and *hute* lavish in the generous forest. At home, there were squashes, pumpkins and *maheu,* especially in summer. Every youth, rich and poor ate until the little tummies bulged and shone dangerously as if they would burst. And, when the youths relieved themselves, they squatted simultaneously at safe distances from each other, safe so that none could watch others anal holes or the stools would refuse to come out. And after the act, as if on cue, everyone would hunt for a thin stick or the leaves of the *muzeze* tree to clean their bottoms. It was those years when the catechist taught her there was a time for everything: a time to be born and a time to die, a time to love and a time to hate…it was all; a life full of opposites. She had learnt that life was full of opposites but had been quick to forget that truth could apply to her too. That was why she had blundered and landed herself in all this mess. Although presently, her mind was a busy hive of hurtling ugly thoughts, she strained herself to face all her challenges squarely in the face.

"If you accidentally meet a hungry lion in the forest unarmed, don't run away. Look squarely into its eyes. It will rise to go," was the *sarungano*—as Shona folk-talers are called. The children believed the *sarunganos* from tender ages when they had drizzling noses, those years when they swam together, boys and girls, in the same pool never noticing their nakedness. Years when sex was sacred, not cheapened by the print and electronic media.

LOOK SQUARELY INTO ITS EYES!

New strength welled in her. And, yet another voice from the past echoed:

"You are going into a hostile world where you will not enjoy the security we have always given you. You are more vulnerable now than never before. You will meet challenges but be prepared to face them all. Never try to run away...."

The voice of a school teacher rang deep in her mind.

FACE THEM!

Face death. Face even her snarling mother-in-law. Oh! how every word she uttered was a bomb. Razors, incising razors that bred gaping, bleeding wounds. Face even the villagers who now celebrated her ultimate downfall. But would he die? Would he ever caress her chin playfully again? Would he....? Would he....? For the tenth time in one hour, her blind right palm took off and landed with astonishing mathematical precision on the left side of the chest to check for the heart-beat. Was he breathing? Was he warm in the arm-pits?

MaMoyo's sky did not begin overcast and stormy. It had the characteristic initial sweet marital moments of sunshine and cloudless blue skies when John and her ate, sat and talked together until the whole village was alive with those disappointing eye-talks.

"WE HAVE BEEN IN LOVE BEFORE BUT THIS....WE WILL SEE WHERE IT ENDS, HOW IT ENDS ..." the eyes whispered. This did not deter the duo at all. Love was in the air. Love was bubbling and springing lavishly. Flowing in every direction.

The secluded Gonye forests and the birds knew them; them and their echoing mirthful laughter. The grass clad river banks knew their secret whispers. But the village women who secretly vied for her company spied them maliciously and waited. *Chinobhururuka chinomhara* – everything has an end they knew. What begins always ends, what flies, lands, what loves will hate? One day in the future. Life is filled with contrasts: God, satan, evil, good, white, black …. But then it was a time of affections, everyone had to accept it.

But what man in his real senses would do that? Wash nappies in broad daylight as MaMoyo perched herself on a stool? What man pounded *mupunga* and roundnuts for a woman who sat and chatted endlessly? What man shunned the company of other men drinking *ndari* from the same gourd chatting, laughing …? Everyone had a score to settle with the duo although their offence was tacit. What man…?

The Guhwa Mountain echoed the question. The air ferried the question. Lips whispered it. The eyes blinked the question. The duo knew the question but what was wrong in all this? "Too traditional!" the duo had fired back. "At times tradition is a stumbling block to real progress. What was wrong for a woman to sit on a stool, chair or sofa? Why insist on her sitting cross-legged on a reed mat? What was the secret behind sitting on a reed mat? What was wrong when a man freely chose to help his partner pound grains with mortar and pestle? Or cook sadza for her? If society did not accept change, the change would change them. Who did not know there were many men sewing clothes in companies? Weren't boys doing Fashion and Fabrics at school? Who cooked sadza and relish in boarding schools? Weren't they bearded men who accepted the dynamics of gender roles in a changing environment? What was wrong keeping company of one's wife? Couldn't people learn from whites? They knew how to love their partners and they marry for themselves not for the damn whole clans or villages. An African woman was communally owned, a community asset with the obligation to please all interested parties. Damn it!

John's family was wrathful and watched the proceedings the way a hungry cat spies at an unconscious rat munching away at a temptingly appetising brown crust. Years of experience had taught them: let things ripen at their pace. Never tamper around with a boil before its time, let it ripen first. Never fast-track the ripening of any fruit, it loses its natural taste. Even friendship for it to be true and lasting, should be a slow ripening thing. Only then can it stand the test of time. The time of fullness, of maturity nearly always came. Naturally!

Little strokes fell great oaks. But what were the strokes? What, who went wrong? The whole thing was an intricate puzzle but all things pointed to the birth of little Ropafadzo. The cracks of the whole thing could have started then. Perhaps because she gave greater time, love and attention to the baby, suckling and talking to it endlessly, fondling it … her man brooding jealously like a weaned child. But he did not complain. She should know it and take corrective measures, he thought. If he complained, he would embarrass himself before her and even the baby: a mature man vying for love and attention with a helpless little being. That should have been the origin of the cracks; a major crack that bore other bigger and more dangerous cracks. Marriage on the rocks.

RIVARLY, VYING WITH A MERE BABY!

Men, drinking men, are never totally sober. They go home drunk, sleep drunk, wake up with hang-over, go to drink again, get drunk, go home drunk, sleep drunk …! John had become part of the village drunkards, mild at first, wild at last. At the zenith of drunken stupor, tongues became dangerously loose. The truth or its exaggerated form, were said in drunken jokes but even in that state, it hurt.

"What has brought you here lame woman of a man? You have run away from washing your wife's underclothes and Ropafadzo's nappies. Who washes them now? Get away from here you foul man …,"was one of the worst village drunkards.

John had hissed back. He was surprised at his anger. Even his drunkenness. And the accurate punches at this opponent. The blood! Where had all these boxing skills been hidden? But John found himself surrounded with showers of blows. He was the odd one out, the sheep for slaughter. But humiliated drunkards have a way of compensating for defeat suffered at beer parties; they vent their fury on defenseless women and children. Equally,

MaMoyo could not take it nor believe it when the first lethal fist landed on her. A dream? A nightmare?

That was when she dared consult the dreaded hideous old woman beyond Rasa Mountain, an unsightly grinning old thing with fiery red eyes, a woman no man ever approached to love. The villagers around, Gonye, Chivasa, Mukiyo, Guramatunhu, Goronga, Chinyaure knew her notoriety. She was nicknamed Terminator. Girls who had unwanted pregnancies paid her homage by the night to get herbs. House-wives with marriage on the rocks thronged her crumbling hut deep in the forest. It is here where her feet had rushed to, where she had received the strange recipe for love. Here, where the cracks of marriage had started widening more. Was the dosage wrong? Was it the right herb, was what what? There was not response, only the womb of darkness with its ominous presence persisted refusing to lift. CRACKS!

*****

9

THE HANDS WE PASSED THROUGH

His car shot along the deserted tarmac like a lone meteor across the pitch blackness of the sky. Clogged at Gonye Township bus stop, was a solid mass of humanity, tired but still waving frantically to stop the few cars which trickled in at lengthy intervals of thirty minutes or so, what with the current fuel shortages bedevilling the nation.

About a hundred meters past the bus stop, he thought he had seen someone, someone uniquely special; so he slowed down and came to a gentle stop. Had he seen well? Was it really him? Did he come from this part of Gutu? Had he indeed resigned as some of his classmates had rumoured? Why would anyone resign at such a time when the economy was at its worst with reports of retirement monies taking decades to be processed? But it could indeed be him since some people said he came from the Vice President's home area where a tarred road was under construction to link the Chivu-Nyazura

10

highway from Gutu Growth Point. He reversed and stopped by the bus stop.

The man he had spotted was past sixty-five years, clad in his characteristic faded safari suit [once popular with people of his profession, but now, because of the fast changing trends in fashion, was an undoubted symbol of lack, backwardness and scorn]. He was shod in cheap unpolished sandals which regrettably, allowed his clean but torn stockings to maliciously sell out some dry, coarse skin patches which cried out unheeded for even the cheapest of the body lotions. On his left shoulder, he slung a zipless satchel bulging threateningly with an assortment of peeping bicycle parts. In his right hand, he clutched two rusty bicycle rims that were bent and certainly needed a bit of straightening up before new spokes could be fitted.

His facial features had crumbled. Then there was the merciless grey hairs that threatened to invade his bald head, eye-lashes and beards with the tenacity and relentlessness of an accomplished aggressive soldier. Only two years of parting with his much loved profession and his life had gotten to this!

Once his car was stationary, the mob broke up and besieged the car, knocking the ageing man to the ground. Faces peeped pleadingly at the driver from every open window, voices chorusing different destinations at once as if the young driver had tens of ears plugged all over his body. "Sorry. Just that man," announced the driver, the engine of his new Mercedes Benz quietly, superiorly, idling.

Dismayed and insulting, the mob retreated to the bus stop and glared accusingly at the driver but who wanted to take risks? You could carry armed robbers and endanger yourself. *Tsitsi dzinotsitstirira*. Kindness can turn against you. Weren't newspapers rife with stories of this nature? You carry strangers at your own risk. You could help the one who would cut your throat and drive away with your car.

The angry sun roasted them adding to their ordeal. They gnashed their teeth, cursing.

"Just petrol! Diesel! Who is causing this? See how much time we waste waving in vain for lifts. You report late for work and the bosses growl at you. Lucky if you are not fired. Who…? Why?

Fuel was like gold. Rare. Scarce. Precious. For a privileged few. The lucky passenger, with a distinct mixture of ultimate triumph, suspense and fear, entered the inviting comfort of the car, sank into the caressing comfort of its seat and gently pulled the back door to a firm shut.

Etiquette! It was requisite even in shutting the doors of important cars like the Benz and the

Citron before it. You didn't bang the doors as if you were shutting the doors of a *sikolokolo* or *mota yaMataka*. Etiquette! They grew with it in their blood. They breathed it. They lived it especially during their youthful days. They practised it when distant relatives visited, when people visited rural relatives at Christmas or New Year. You behaved well even if you used to be restless and talkative. If you were a boy, you crouched in greeting. Girls knelt and shyly looked on the ground unlike the emerging uncultured boys who stand like gum trees when greeting elders and the girls who look unflinchingly and directly in an elder's eyes until you turn your gaze away in defeat. Just a few minutes earlier, had he not been knocked down by some youths as everyone vied for transport to their respective destinations? Didn't one beardless youth trample over him and never said even an insincere apology to appease him. Bastards!

Thud! Thud! His pounding heart reminded him he was in a stranger's car. Wasn't there a *tokoloshe* or weird snake in the basket next to him? Wasn't there a huge sharp knife read to slice him open? What lurked under the seat covers? And the boot? If his head was cut off...! But why had man's heart become fierce jungles like that? It was said all beheaded human heads went South in exchange for kombis. Weird, wild, world. The dignity of working and sweating ... all dead and buried!

The car sped on. Silence reigned. Who should talk first, the passenger quizzed himself. The guest or the host? The silence needed to be broken. It was just stifling. Involuntarily, he croaked a tremulous "Morning *chef*." The driver was momentarily mum for lack of an appropriate response.

Etiquette! Who endorsed that elders could cheaply, shamefully, trade their dignity and self-worth for a paid ride for that matter? Who endorsed this stinking culture that grey-haired octogenarians should put their hats off for their own children with milk not yet dry on their baby noses? Who? When? It was happening all over. At funerals, smoke and sweat -smelling elders abandoned their wooden stools for smartly turned up town boys in collar and tie. How on withered bottoms they sat on gravelly soils. Who in the holy book sold his birth right for a plate of ....! Was it peas or beans? The priest at Mutero Mission knows better. But it was for something worthless and trivial. Who? What was compromising on etiquette? The youthful generation? The elderly? A combination of both? Who...? What...? When...? Where...? The car sped on.

Muscles! The one with the muscle got respect. Age used to have muscles and the youths would salute every elder they came across. Those years, every elderly person was honoured and respected and had the tacit permission to discipline any misbehaving child, anywhere, anytime. Nowadays everyone speaks of different muscles. Political muscle! Financial muscle! Bookish muscle! Legal muscle! They are the thieves of honour and respect.

Financial muscle! One could see it in times of death or misfortune. Clueless, elderly rural people fold their hands on their backs and announce: "Did you call the boys or girls in town? Wait for them. Things will be sorted out in the twinkling of an eye once they arrive." Even in times of peace, the financial muscle is felt. A son- in- law who visit his in-laws by car attracts more respect and honour than the one who visits walking in car tyre sandals. People have different values and value systems. Death of a culture!

"I'm your blood *baba*," came the lethal bomb at last, throwing fiery bits into his face, bruising him. "You saw the sun first before me. You carried us on your loving shoulders as you went to herd cattle or visit the distant fields. You taught us life at home and later sent us to school. Nothing short of pride can elevate us above you. It is you who empowered us to climb the social ladder. We owe much to you. I owe you much, especially you! Mr Tsuro." The man started. Mouth agape. Eyes like huge inflated balls "Ah!" the passenger exclaimed. The driver smiled at the passenger's theatrical reaction. "So you are going to fix the bicycle parts to beat the transport blues? Did you not get the retirement package to buy a *sikolokolo baba*?" Both laughed heartily.

Who didn't know the retirement forms took years before being processed as if the process was done by aliens overseas? Who really brooded over people's forms like a hen sitting on eggs? Who sat on people's papers when they had kids to send to school and feed? Who brooded on people's papers when they needed decent clothes and rentals? Was this their due for loyal service and dedication? How many souls had gone through the hands of this man travelling with him? The hands people went through needed respect and honour and due acknowledgement.

The car wheels turned and turned. Unceasingly. Fast. "Who are you son?" the passenger asked curiously? You know by the nature of my previous profession many souls pass through our hands. It's a mammoth task to remember every name…"

"Am one of those who revelled in your brightness about ten years ago. You were the selfless candle which burnt itself out so that we could realise these dizzying social and economic heights. You sacrificed a lot, guided and counselled us as your own biological children. I'm now a doctor at the mission hospital. Are you aware that you bore several doctors, pharmacists, engineers..? Tonight you should put up at my place so that I can tell it all."

The car turned left and stopped at the mission hospital gate. The passenger shifted on the car seat and wondered, a new sense of pride, self-worth and self-confidence creeping back into him. Candles! Selfless candles! Dumped candles! Scorned and abandoned gold mines!

"Only Germany has realised their worth and pays them handsomely...no one earns more than them for everyone passes through their hands...," were the angry words the wind carried to a place no one knew.

*****

THE CONSEQUENCES

When they caught a glimpse of the boy through chinks on their kitchen door, they were engrossed in eating their lunch of *sadza* and bitter *munyivhi* void of any drop of cooking oil or peanut butter, so they both felt the sharp sting of the relish on their tongues; one reason why they yearned to see their boy complete his studies at high school and proceed to university.

True, their kraal that once breathed with fat oxen and heifers was empty. To get solace, they had used every log for fire. To burn away every nasty thought of the past; bury tormenting thoughts.

Tears! Men should never cry and every crying man is labelled a woman in men's clothes. But he, the father of the house, had shed tears in broad daylight. Not over a dead child or parent. Or relative. To be exact, he had cried ten times and the whole Gonye village had nicknamed him "Misodzi"—meaning tears and "Dera"—a true coward. It was not a small thing watching butcherman driving away his beasts away for slaughter—beasts he had herded in the snake—infested Ruzhezha and Guhwa mountains. Beasts he had herded in *mvura yembambara* – those fierce storms. Beasts he could have killed to appease his rebellious appetites. The butcher men! They dumped bank notes like that on his lap, rose and began to drive the beasts away. Just like that. Never to see the beasts again. Never to hear their knowing mooing or bellowing when he visited the kraal and fed them from his work-tortured palms. All in a bid to educate a soul.

He cried. Quietly though. But crying is crying.

The gods ultimately smiled at him and the former dark sinister clouds of despair bade him goodbye as the boy excelled at high school. "Our kraal will be full one day," Mai Tindo solaced her husband. "Beyond every upland, there is a lowland. Time flies Baba Tindo. We will smile one day. One day, all our scorners will dance, the dance of triumph and jubilation with us. Mark my words."

A bit perturbed, Baba Tindo throws his morsel into the plate and heads for the door. How could the boy come back home from school on the opening day? Were the rumours true then? The rumours of the previous term. "*Kwakanaka here?* Is everything well son?" he asks when the boy is in the yard. Silence. "Is it about the last term's unfinished fees? Your headmaster knows I pay him after harvesting my crop of beans or maize or after selling a beast...." Utter silence. The boy just advances, eyes red and teary. The rumour! Last term's rumour! "Speak son," coaxes mother in a tremulous voice, "Answer your father." Tindo charges into the kitchen and throws himself on the dung-polished earthen bench and looks on the dung smeared floor, eternally averting his parents' inquisitive eyes. "The head wants you," he bellows uncomfortably. "In connection with?" fires the man of the house? "They said I ...."

Baba Tindo recalls that day when he was about to reach for the nestling up the *Mushumha* tree and his very friend pulled him down by the shirt. Pulled him down completely. The nestling flew away and both of them lost out. That was during his childhood days.

Son of mine, what unforgivable treachery. How could you do that? Inciting

21

others to strike over eating sadza with vegies. You grew up here in the rural area eating *chirevereve*, *mubvunzandadya*, and *nyivhi*. Do you eat better food here? You ate sadza with crickets or sugar and salt solution—*nhongamuto*. You never complained! You ate and your tummy bulged. You thanked us. We received your thanks. You should have put your priorities right son. Does higher education blind? Knowledge, does it blind the mind? We thought we were opening up your mind, little did we know we were doing you wrong.

You break the windows and doors over food. Tindo my son! You led others in rebellion. Will the head understand me? Will they ever accommodate you at the boarding school? You have killed us both. Even your siblings who have gone to school. You dared skin us alive, son.

And the beasts we sold? And the tears I shed? Today our jealous neighbours will rejoice. They will celebrate. And this issue of meeting girls in dark corners…. There are village girls here. If you needed girls. Marwei is dying for you here. Chipo and Rudo too. We are exposed. How shall we face the world? Your Head too?

Son, I was a student once. I saw athletes who ran laps well and fainted a few centimetres from the winning line. A miss is as good as a mile. You know Mr Tambo well, don't you? For decades he served his company faithfully but lost all his benefits after stealing a packet of nails. Nails! And destinies are destroyed. *Chirongo chinorema munhu wosvika* — burdens get heaviest when destinations are just a stone's throw. You know how spiteful the women of this village are. They will do anything to provoke me. To hurt. To offend. We will no longer fetch water at the village borehole. We can't. How like a village leper have become? Son, your father's tears at the sale of each beast.... Our back-aches after each long day's weeding! Our calloused, work-tortured hands ... They should have reminded you of our ultimate sacrifice...!

Shouldn't education liberate the mind? You are now like Madenda, that educated professor who runs away from his electricity — lit houses to be with stinking uneducated bitches in candle lit shacks. Son ... !

*****

23

BEFORE I DIE

A real man shouldn't just die like one of the wretched dogs: dying without leaving something; skills, knowledge or property for posterity. It is unforgivable sin and your children's children will forever point accusingly and insultingly at your grave years after you are gone. "The man who lies there, bore us to suffer. Our family woes started from him," every generation will say.

As I prepare to join my ancestors, anytime from now, I wouldn't like to be like Maruza, the herbalist. Am sure six years after his death, all our ancestors are judging him daily, condemning him for dying like a dog.

Who in the district of Gutu knew how to cure every snake-bite more than Maruza? Who knew herbs that cured various ailments more than him? He intimately knew where herbs grew in the thick forest, mountain summits and under the deep waters. He had the monopoly of the vast knowledge and never shared a bit of his inexhaustible secrets with his brother, nor his dearest son, Dzotso. What stinginess! That is why I maintain he is under terrible judgment by offended ancestors who see their children torn into pieces by the hawks of life because of the egoism of a man.

Knowledge and skills possessed should be knowledge and skills shared for the benefit of prosperity. As I lie here, all alone like the island, there are many things I am dying to share with the people of this great country. Don't allow our languages to die. All our languages. Languages of the land, Shona, Ndebele, Kalanga, Tonga ... The language of the strangers is needful but should not tower and straddle over ours. Whose language is frequently used in schools and work places? I hear in schools students who use their local mother tongue language are punished severely to teach them a good lesson that their mother tongues should die. For identifying with their culture, they are made to clean the messed up toilets. And, the day they speak the stranger's languages, their teachers and parents applaud uproariously for them. Death of a culture!

Our proverbs and idiomatic expressions are taught in a very superficial way to make students pass their examination. And the citizens of this great nation, who has told you to stop creating more of those proverbs; proverbs tailor-made for different social eras to reflect our experiences. Have we stopped experiencing life?

Why can't we create proverbs like: *Tezvara mukwashawo kumwe*? The father- in- law is also someone's son- in–law? It is a witty saying that would rebuke callous and insensitive fathers- in- law to empathise with their sons- in- law and exercise love and tolerance towards them. Another proverb: *Seri kwemukwidza materu* – beyond every highland is a lowland. This would strengthen people to face life's challenges knowing perfectly well that every hardship is sure to pass by and give way to peace and joy.

This is my worry as I lie on the mat. Everyone has gone to the fields – I told them to go and weed. Monitoring me will not bring *manhanga*, *nyimo* and *makavhu* on the table. They complied and went and I have a good time alone reflecting on worthwhile issues.

And our traditional childhood games. They have wilted and died in the sun. Our children don't know *kusika nyimo* – spinning round nuts on a *guyo*–flat rock platform. They can't tell the types of *nyimo* like *svundu, gunguwo, dahwa* and *musodzi*. They know how to cook and eat roundnuts but lack deep knowledge about them. Even some of our professors don't possess this basic information. Even our water games haven't been spared. *Hero sadzamukuche,* for instance. Our children should know we swam with girls in the same pool. Girls with full breast! Naked! No report of mischief ever reached the ears of adults. Our children should be taught that it's possible for sexes to mix responsibly. Today our youths see naked women in books, on the televisions and their phones and masturbate! I hear they keep pictures of naked women or boys in those phones. Death of *unhu*.

I have ten more issues I have to pour out from my troubled heart but my right side is now aching. I have to roll myself and lie with the left side. But that will take a while. Meanwhile, get your pens and papers. I have quite a lot to share with everyone before I die.

*****

THE HARBINGER

Never had Billy Benon been so sore disenchanted. He never stopped wondering why the black guard could have broken such prickly news to his already apprehensive, ageing parents. The most sensible thing would have been for him to inform him so that he, in turn, could have sought a more euphemistic way of breaking the news. To torture him and to show disapproval, Billy just invaded the grovelling Pundo with his unblinking eyes.

"Sorry, Baas!" Pundo said facing down eternally like a wooed African girl. Billy later joined his parents who were painstakingly screwing up their blurring eyes to spot the intruder.

"Black ruffian, Billy. So I 've heard," Mr Benon said. "Land –grabbers!" shrieked Clarie.

In no time, Billy had bought the binoculars to confirm the spectacle. At first, he could see the crude grass-and-tree branch shelter a kilometre away by the gate, next to the main tarred road. Then he saw an object moving up and down in the carpet of towering thatching grass. It was a person's head.

"He is probably digging. Has been there for some time now, I reckon. He has thrown up a structure," Billy reported still looking intently at the same spot. We need to be cautious lest we worsen the situation. You know the Marondera incident that culminated in death? We've to avoid that. Land can be bought not life. If the worse comes to worst, we can always approach the police, Billy warned. The couple just looked on.

"Billy don't be so tame! Remember this is your inheritance. We will drive there. We have to speak with the intruder," Mr Benon said shaking and mouth foaming piteously. Billy watched the dimming and blackening countenances of his parents and wished the Svosve people were never put on the face of the earth after all. "They started it, he accused," he accused.

The intruder had arrived here previous two days and had gone on to erect a temporary shelter. From the very first day, he had dug with prodigious energy. Rarely did he rest or look sideways. He just faced the black soils and secretly talked to it.

"I'm no alien here. I know the secret songs of this land. I speak the language of this land. My umbilical cord belongs here and is in this soil…

I know the smell of blood and the groaning of the dying soldier as he fought for you mother land. We fed from tree leaves, crouching. We co-existed with the game to reclaim you. The *povo*, oh those people! They fed us and clothed us. They exhorted us. Comforted us. Some died for you and their gushing blood lavishly watered you. The *povo! Viva povo!* See their gaping kraals for they supported Chimurenga Two. *Viva Mujibha! Viva Chimbwidos! Viva* war vets*!*

We won the war to settle on you. Twenty years the goods were not delivered. In Chipinge, they still dwell on hills and rocks like rock rabbits. They reap the wind. Elsewhere, they farm the sandy or rocky soils and reap weeds. They mourn, your children. They fight amongst themselves for boundaries. It's not time for that but time to be the Svosve people.

Chimurenga Three, has come. We cannot forget the fighters. Your valiant, selfless sons who braved the deluge of rains and cold rushing winds. We cannot forget those who stood by us. They can't all be paid in cash for this will kill our economy. Let them have you mother earth so that they can create wealth forever…."

He gripped the mattock handle firmly and continued to plough the soil. He felt it; the breaking of every resistance of the hard soil. His trickling sweat seemed to water it, soften it. Every tuft of the grass or bush along the way got bulldozed. It pleased him; being a bulldozer. Had he not risen to rest a while, he could have remained oblivious of the approaching car which later parked beside his shelter.

Ignoring it, he surveyed the vast piece he had dug with his own hands. He was mum and provocatively resumed digging, this time with demoniac energy. He never listened. Did not want to see anything other than the soil and his mattock. And his dripping sweat. Then something poked him.

"I say again get out right away or face this!" a white figure said. The mattock-bearer calmly rose to look at it. He laughed a bitter, scornful laugh. After spitting in his hands and rubbing them against each other to improve his grip, he bent to resume digging. By some miracle, he found himself on the ground, the mattock meters away. A hulk of a man stood astride him breathless and fuming. "No, dad! Is that dialogue? Is that what we agreed on?" a young white man who came running from the stationary Land rover pleaded. "Get off my land!" Mr Benon thundered again.

"Who are you on this land?" Morari said at last still lying down. "Your land? To be clear enough, you are a land-grabber. This is our land. This is the black man's. You can as well plead with me to allow you a portion. Your workers, Baas, need land too. They will get their share here soon".

Mr Benon lifted his massive right leg to trample on him. Billy was fast enough. He held his father's leg mid-air forcing him to fall. Morari rose up determinedly and soon the giant and the small giant were locked up in a fierce wrestling. Billy tried to pacify them in vain.

Just then, there was a drone in the distance. Soon, a lorry laden with shouting and sloganeering mob slowed down and turned towards the gate. The oblivious wrestlers battled on. Only Billy and the mob had seen each other. As soon as the mob saw it, they jumped out of the lorry and swarmed towards the scene cursing.

*****

CAUGHT UP IN THE BATTLE

The Masvingo City clock struck one p.m. and abruptly, the crowded, sweat-drenched, shovelling and cursing humanity discontinued their struggle for a brief moment as if a strict referee has blown his whistle for the madness to be called off. It was an unusual August 2003teachers' pay day during the school holiday. For these warriors, the time had flown without them noticing it. So, when the big clock sounded, they opened their dry-lipped mouths widely in disbelief.

They had stood in the thickening "thing" for over five good hours; how could one call it a queue when they all huddled together like chicks on a bitterly cold night? The initial neat queue experienced at seven in the morning before banks opened, had mysteriously bulged at every point. I smelt trouble for all prospects of travelling back to Munyikwa were slim. The thick "thing" remained stagnant although at intervals, one surly-looking guard took scores of clients into the banking hall. There was no way it could really subside when every late-comer claimed to have been standing in the queue ahead of or behind so and so. Tempers had already flared and everyone tacitly knew that the volatile atmosphere needed no etiquette. The solution was pressing hard on trespassers until they opted out of the queue. The plan nearly always worked.

Then someone shocked us again; the maximum withdrawal had once more been reduced to a mere two thousand Zimbabwean dollars from the initial ten thousand dollars. The cash in the bank was said to be running out fast but what could that amount serve to clients who had spent several thousand dollars on bus fare to Masvingo? The already fatigued and hungry militants were further infuriated and cursed with obscenities at no person in particular. The curses later on turned into low murmurings but since hunger and thirst had taken their toll, everyone was quiet again and concentrated on pushing and shoving.

I was one of the actors in the "queue", drowned in the middle of it. Readers will probably sympathise with me knowing well that I am slim and dwarfish. I was mercilessly sandwiched and was gasping and groaning like one of Sekuru Mandebvu's diseased chicks.

"Let me have a way out!" I yelled breathlessly, resignedly. I had put up my utmost in the protracted battle. That was the furthest I could remain in combat and had reached the limits of endurance. Alas for me, it wasn't the right time to appeal for attention or mercy for everyone had ceased hearing and every grain of pity or compassion had deserted human hearts. I was mesmerised. Here was a desperate situation that defied courtesy or etiquette. Women squeezed against men, satchels against breasts, breasts against hands …anything against anything. None complained. Money!

"Here is jungle life unfolding before me," I lamented. The compact mass persisted around me when suddenly, a plan struck me. Desperate situations demanded desperate solutions, I had learnt. Like a rabid bull, I jabbed anyone close by with my pointed elbows. The plan seemed to work. The victims stirred with a jerk, just cursing. I capitalised on this golden chance. I sank low and started worming myself through the seemingly unending network of legs. Of course, I received vicious kicks for that. After what seemed eternity, safety was reached. Free at last, but physically spent, I crawled a few metres away from the battle-ground and watched the unabated drama with new awe.

Young mothers with whispering babies precariously strapped on their backs soldiered in the battle for money; the money they had laboured for. This another battle; a battle to withdraw it. I laughed to myself when I realised that I had probably been one of the most comic actors in the drama the past few minutes.

The baking sun didn't relent as its hostile rays landed with lethal stings on unprotected sweating foreheads. I was hurt. I scrutinised my suit. It was stained with dirt. Three buttons of the jacket were missing. The tie had dropped out of my pocket and I could see it being trampled by hostile and unheeding feet. I cursed and the wind carried the words to a place I didn't know.

The corrupt guards and tellers contributed to this mess. Who didn't know they were bribed? The guards allowed clients to take front positions in the queue at a cost. Wasn't it rumoured too that the tellers gave their relatives and "special" clients bigger amounts of 20 000? And wasn't it true that if their friends wanted bank cheques, they were processed within a matter of two hours when everyone else got the amount after at least a day.

Favouritism! Corruption.

I resisted the urge to barge into the hall to assault the guards, tellers and management. The tellers especially, for I heard they deliberately served the clients slowly to get paid for overtime. My rumbling tummy reminded me I was famished and hadn't taken anything to pacify it. I fumbled in my pockets and fished out two five hundred dollar notes.

"That's enough for a few buns and a very cold Fanta. After such a struggle, it would be a good reward," I pronounced as I dragged my feeble and aching legs towards the Indian woman's take-away close to ZIMBANK. But why here, at ZIMBANK, in spite of the cash shortages, clients got as much as forty thousand dollars?

The Indian woman served me fast with a commercial smile all over her face .I was hungry and couldn't smile back. It was quite regrettable. My once painful legs miraculously carried me towards the Civic Centre at a brisk pace. I fumbled for the opener in my bag and finding none, thought of improvising. My teeth were the nearest God-given tools at hand. First time, and they had removed the bottle-top. There was no waste of time. I sank my teeth into the first bun, chewed and had a quick gulp of the invitingly cold Fanta. I was choked and little tears formed in my eyes. I was gratified that the incident would not make any news for it seemed no one nearby knew me nor cared about what was happening to me. So, I wiped my eyes with the back of my palm and resumed feeding by this time reminding myself that I was a teacher after all. Satisfied, I lay on my back and heaved a sigh. I had five hundred dollars left in my pocket.

Invigorated by now, I scurried back to the banking hall. That wretched 'queue' was still there but the tugging had ceased. Clients just stood there wearing desperate faces. The bank had run out of cash and clients would have to be served next day. Slowly, as we approached seven p.m. people began to disperse and the banking hall was closed. With the lodges charging at least ten thousand dollars per night, I knew perfectly well that I would put up in the queue. I was third in the queue and hoped that the next morning, I would be served earlier. Surely, I had gone to the city for pay not this battle.

***** 2003 – days of money shortage in most Zimbabwean banks*****

THE COLONISED MIND

You're a keen farmer who grows crops and hopes to reap bountifully. You don't sow weeds, but you know that wild seeds are there unseen and waiting maliciously in the soil. They are always there uninvited waiting to sprout, grow and compete for space, air, nutrients and sunlight with your plants. Soon, your plants germinate and begin to flourish. The weeds too. You begin to watch in utter horror as the weeds begin to outgrow the legitimate plants. They slowly but surely begin to colonise the field and uncompromisingly choke your plants. Your plants can hardly be seen, only the tops pleading and peeping for attention. You hear the cry of your plants, quickly brew beer and call for a *humwe*. You are relieved as your weeded plants freely and gently dance in the breeze. The weeds lie wilting in the merciless heat. Yes, a field colonised by the weeds requires a *humwe*. I sometimes think my troubled mind needs a *humwe* – concerted effort too. So many wise advisors, counsellors and friends who can help me realise a complete mental revolution.

Frankly speaking, I grew up with the burning desire to marry. My first choice would be a nurse, the second a teacher. I would marry from the envied professions, for during the 1970s, we admired teachers and nurses, especially nurses because one musicians sang positively about them. The song went: "*Mwoyo yenyu yakachena kunge mwedzi wechirimo, manesi.*" (Nurses, your hearts are sublime). My prospective wife should have such a loving and caring heart. I remember scorning priests or nuns. Why did they pretend to have miraculously dropped from heaven when they were fruits of married couples? Why did they want other married people's children to serve them in various ways when they did not want their own children? Why did they preach to other people's children? Why not preach to trees, stones, lizards, ants and the wind? That was my line of thinking then. I hated priesthood and wanted to marry later in life.

But now when the time to marry knocks, I begin to shudder. I am afraid I can't fully explain the origin of this fear. You know, I am in love for the tenth time over a period of five years. I have been in deep love but in all cases, I have failed to take the next crucial step:

marriage. Every time I think of the word, I feel stifled, squashed. I feel I'll be about to give away something valuable, indispensable and in turn get grief, sorrows and regrets. I feel I'll be giving away my freedom, imprisoning myself eternally… And nearly every time I'm about to commit myself, the idea of marrying a woman whose body has been explored through and through by other men haunts me. Explored lands and seas present no excitement to adventurers. It feels suicidal like one plunging into a fathomless sea from which there is utterly no escape. Now I just can't trust any woman fully. In fact, I believe there aren't many virgins left in the world. At times, I try to suppress all these ideas but then there are those words spoken by someone I have forgotten: "Never ever marry Chinoda. Learn from my mistakes. These days people don't marry wives but knives …" These words haunt me every time I have a serious affair. These are the words that have colonised my mind. But who is the owner of these words? When were the words spoken and where? What was the context by the way? I think I now remember!

I was scurrying home after work so that I could somehow reward myself with a bit of rest. With the characteristic power- cuts in the city, I needed a decent hot meal and of course, attend to some laundry or once again risk going to work dressed in creased clothes and appear like one of those horrible scarecrows in groundnut fields. This would not augur well for a bachelor like me, someone still looking around for a prospective lover. Clothes, I believed, had the magnetism to attract the 'birds' of the opposite sex.

That day was part of the routine unbroken stream of pedestrians footing briskly to Majange towards sunset. (Few people boarded kombis, what with the sky-rocketing fares). I heard a distinct voice and on looking closely, caught sight of a skeletal figure weakly beckoning at me. I could not make out who the stranger was. So, I scurried on indifferently. A moment later, a hand gripped me on my right shoulder the way a police officer may grip a culprit attempting to escape. I stopped abruptly in my way and shot a perplexed and inquisitive glare at the stranger who appeared immediately amused by my theatrical reaction. "Can I be of any help?" I barked, frowning.

The slim figure just dished out a lavish smile that stubbornly remained in his seemingly youthful yet surprisingly denuded facial terrain. Did he know I was in such a hurry? Did he know town people tend to have no second to waste on trivial issues – they are nearly always busy-hurrying? Always behind time, they seem. Always too busy for casual talk.

"Chinoda! Still alive?" the broomstick of a man asked familiarly. I smiled back to save myself from an embarrassment for failing to recognize a person who appeared to know me well. Gradually, it dawned on me that the smile was Tanaka's, but the physical appearance was not his, at least as far as I could remember. That was the puzzle at hand. I had to unblock. "Tanaka!" I guessed.

He nodded his characteristic smile dancing on his dark course face. "But why my dear friend? Three years of separation and you have become this? What happened to you? What is actually happening?" I asked.

In answer, he led me away a few paces from the swarming homebound workers. Away from workers, Tanaka fixed me with eyes that seemed to preach doom. "Still alive too? He asked contorting his creased face with disbelief. I nodded.

"You are lucky. Never ever marry. Learn from my mistakes. These days, people marry knives not wives..." Tears had taken better of him. When he had calmed down, he went on with his sad narration. "You remember the rural girl I married about five years ago, sent to night school and uplifted? You remember, she had only one "O" Level pass in Shona? I struggled and at last she had five "O" Level passes. I later sent her to college and the very first month in college bad reports began to trickle in. I heard that she, with several other married women, had thrown away their wedding rings. She was flirting with young college mates who called her by her first name. I could not believe it. I heard that posh cars came by evening to pick her up to places no one knew. What transpired at those places, God knows. This was just hearsay, but you know I later caught her red-handed doing 'it' with an ugly bald-headed man, the age of her father, a rich business man.

"I mean red-handed…! I divorced her but she went to the courts to claim for maintenance. How could I maintain a child I doubted was my own blood? I could quit teaching and go abroad. Or even stay at home doing any menial work rather than maintain the child. But, does that help? I can feel something eating my flesh away. This is the fruit of my zeal to develop my wife. I repeat, never ever marry or you will marry a knife not a wife. It is terrible to live for years with regrets."

That was part of the sad story whose influence on me was great. That is why I can't fully trust anyone or if I try to trust or love, I cannot marry anyone. I cannot commit myself especially as stories of infidelity abound in marriages. That is my conclusion. I know that can be a fallacy but I have grown to accept it. I am a prisoner because of other people's words and experiences. Words, ideas, experiences, I believe can be mental colonialists and am the colonized. Can someone help?

*****Written in 2006 before ARVs were available in Zimbabwe*****

LABOUR PAINS

Time! Time kills. Time heals. At least from what we were watching on our television screen, I concluded that time is a little flickering flame that can slowly but surely burn away memories. It is a fathomless grave where living memories die and rot. That is perhaps why I had forgotten. That is why you had probably forgotten too. In life, we tend to forget yesterday's pangs of pains because of present joys. We sometimes, too, forget past joys because of present heaviness and sorrows.

The lamenting former fighter—a female war veteran for that matter—made me think of a pregnant woman who brings a new soul into this world. Soon, so soon, she forgets those indescribable pains soothed by the sight of the baby charmingly wriggling and bubbling with life and vigour in her warm lap. How easily she forgets the pains that beget the present smiles. I had lost memory too. I had sadly forgotten.

In the midst of the interview, the weeping former fighter at least reminded every Zimbabwean that the peace, joy and prosperity that we revel in today are all sweet babies of yesterday's sweat, sacrifice, and bloodbath. Someone, a man or a woman, boy or girl, alive or deceased, able- bodied or physically challenged, healthy or ailing, paid the dear price.

I watched intently as clouds of tears slowly formed and condensed in her eyes. The next moment, bitter tears cascaded down her light cheeks. She cried from the heart–a bruised, bleeding heart. I was hurt at heart. It was a heart to heart communication between a people who had both once tasted the bitter dish of war; she had been a freedom fighter and I was a youthful *mujibha*– a war collaborator.

New Ziana always brought us war time experiences every Saturday evening and my little boys had fallen in love with the programmes which showcased thrilling "fiction." This evening, two female and one male war-veterans appeared on our screens recounting war experiences. It was the stouter lady who touched my heart most. "… Some of us could not proceed with our education because we had gone to war. We are happy, however, that at least our people can pluck the fruits of our toil and efforts. Some are now prominent business persons or professionals. The land, which was at the core of our struggle, has been given back to its rightful owners. What is heart-rending is the fact that some of our people have become a thorn in the flesh. Some of them bluntly tell us that going to war was out of choice and not by compulsion. To that end, there is little or no acknowledgement or recognition of us as liberators …We appeal to our people to accept us for what we are so that we can fit into society more readily …"

That was part of the speech that made her cry. For the first time in twenty-six years, I really felt obliged. Obliged to recount to my two boys what I could about the war-veterans. The tears of the female war-veteran had provided fertile ground for a serious discussion that evening.

"Little children, all the war features you see on television are no funny fabrications or the Hare and Baboon tales meant to entertain and educate youths as they sit around evening fires. The freedom fighters paid dearly for the independence that everyone else now enjoys.

'As a young *mujibha* back in the early 1979, I used to mingle with them in the dark forests where they hid by day and by night. Some of them were man and women in their thirties or forties. Others were boys and girls who could have been at secondary school or university. They lived away from their respective homes and co-existed with the game like wild animals. Theirs was a passion to see all oppressed blacks emancipated.

'In their forest bases, they talked avidly about the various encounters with the Rhodesian soldiers. Now and again, they had a chance to sing and dance all the while alert just in case. One day, in September 1979, they sang madly as independence was knocking at our doors. The song went:

Hona Zanu waiona

Hona Zanu vakomana

Hona Zanu chiwororo

Hona bato revatema

Topinda muHarare

Takubata magidi edu

Hona Zanu waiona!

It was a song in praise of a political party then led by Mr R.G Mugabe. It expressed their dream to tread the streets of Harare triumphantly, brandishing their guns in celebration. Some died before the great day of independence away from their families, lovers and villages.

At times, they killed the enemy but they got killed too. I remember when four comrades lost their lives at Dhliwayo Farm in Mujumba's Wiltshire farms. About a week later, at least three freedom fighters were ambushed at Goronga Farm. They died tragically and the local farmers buried them in shallow graves among dense Msasa forests. The local farmers were the few silent mourners. The fighters' parents or relatives were all the while oblivious of their sons and daughters' fate.

That is why the female character you saw on our screens wept. She knows the birth pains of our independence. To be held with contempt or disrespect after such a nasty experiences calls for sorrowful tears.

Do you know the comrades at times drank their own urine to pacify their thirst? Do you know at times, they went for days without food? Do you know too, that at times they ate tree roots or barks to quieten their hungers?

"One day there were hundreds of them at uncle Mavedzenge's farm in 1979. An ox was slaughtered for them but the plates were in short supply. We had to dish the *sadza* on tree branches and leaves and the relish on the available plates. I watched painfully as they crouched and ate ravenously and contentedly. They thought that perhaps one day they would be able to eat relaxedly when freedom was born.

That day they sang a sad song that summarised their condition. It went:

Ndo patigere pano baba

Ndo patigere pano

Mvura ikauya inongotinaya baba

Mhepo ikauya inotivhuvhuta baba

Ndo patigere pano!

The song said it all; the torrents of rain poured on them in the forests, the hostile gales smote them but they endured the harsh weather conditions. They did not mind the pains, the sweat, and the drudgery as long as the child of their labour would materialise.

"Little boys don't you think the freedom fighters are like the proverbial selfless candles which burn themselves out so that others can enjoy their light." Don't you think too that they are like the generous ladder that has enabled many Zimbabweans to climb their way to great heights of prosperity? What if the inmates curse the candle for its brightness and the ladder for its generosity?"

I could have gone on and on. I could have told them about outstanding exploits of comrades John Zvoushe, Solo, Themba, Modern and Simukai of Chivhu and comrades Chando and Mabhunumuchapera of Gutu. I hope next time I will but for now, I was glad I had at least told them about the labour pains.

*****Inspired by a feature of New Ziana
12 March 2006*****

EMPTINESS

The day I replied grandma that milk came from the bottle, she laughed until she cried. From that day onwards, father vowed to take us to the rural areas every school holiday.

"That's where our roots are. After all, the air there is clean and most things natural and original," father had reassured me.

True to his word, we found every holiday both eventful and educative. In summer, grandma took us around. She patiently told us the names of different mushrooms and the various environments they flourish. She spontaneously composed a song about their names. "*Ruzutwe, firifiti, jongwe, zheveyambuya, nhedzi, bandapakutu, dindindi, hwowamatanda* …," her voice rang. She employed the same tactic for the names of the plants that formed traditional relish: "*chirevereve, mumanga, nyivhi, munhenzva, muboora, musungusungu* …" At a glance, we could differentiate between a *mugake* and *mubvunzandadya*, plants that look nearly alike.

With the aid of fellow rural friends, we began to be more adventurers. Grandma just looked and winked at our parents as if to say, "See how your children have fallen in love with the rural areas. Their roots."

I remember one day, Taru spotted a mudfish-hokota—in a small pool. We knew it was not all alone. There could be several more fish in the murky waters. We found our little palms scooping out the water for a good three hours! Then we saw them, the frightened confused creatures wriggling, trapped by the hostile sand. We caught twenty *miramba* and *machenja* and scurried home eager to receive praise from grandma. The way she ululated. It made one wish to do good things every time. That day, she ululated and danced. Ululated and said our praise poem. It was the first time for me to know that each totem had its unique praise poem:

"Maita Shoko

Makwiramiti

Vadyivezvokuba

MaitaMukanya …," her voice rang out.

Now in Form Two, I see this event with anew eye. We scooped the pool and left the fish exposed, vulnerable. This time, it's not the fish, it's me, Ropafadzo, the daughter of Mr and Mrs Murawo. A mysterious giant hand is scooping everything around me and I feel very frightened, insecure, and confused. Especially because no one chooses to open up and tell me the truth of what is happening around me.

Imagine father and mother hug me in the morning as I leave for school calling me their little angel. In the evening things have changed. Father finds me watching my favourite television programme. I rise up to allow him to hug me as usual. He just brushes me aside as if I am a rotten stinking something. Mother who sits close to me, just pops out her eyes in shock. He remains in the bedroom and calls for his supper to be brought by the maid in that gruffly voice that makes one shudder. I miss his usual laughter and fat jokes. I just sit still, wondering, blinking stupidly, and waiting for an explanation of what is happening around me.

Two days later, my breakfast changes! Cold milk and cornflakes, toasted bread, eggs and tea are replaced with plain porridge. It refused to go down my throat. It just can't. Mother begins to drift. She is reserved, secretive and sullen. I want to ask but the way she glares at me. Where was her usual warmth migrated to? What has caused this unwelcome migration?

Then one day I overhear the man who comes with the company car saying to father, "You are lucky Mr Murawo. You should have been arrested. Embezzlement of company funds is a very terrible offence." I looked up the word in dictionary and had a clue of father's offence." Mom remained mum.

The next thing, the company car that ferries me to and from school is gone and I have to walk to the bus stop to wait for the dreaded kombis. What an ordeal! The conductor shoves me in and commands to squeeze in on the seat. He remains standing, stooping in fact so that he breathes directly into my face. What a breath! His arm-pits exude a foul, sweaty odour that makes one faint. I frown.

"Some people want to be smart for nothing. This is a kombi, not your father's private car," he insults. I know he means me. All eyes are glued on me. I blush. Now, I've accepted my situation but still wonder what is scooping things around me. Why am I suffering in the dark like this? Where is the family bliss? Where are all the endearments?

Today, the maid says she is going back to her place. Father can no longer afford to pay her $80 per month. I watch her pack silently, meditatively and leave, tears cascading down her cheeks. I know she is not prepared to leave. Everything has taken her by surprise. I accompany her, poor soul and leave her at the gate. She hugs me and walk away with her two bags.

I can predict what follows. Tomorrow morning, I will wake up as early as 5am to clean the house, wash the dishes and prepare my plain porridge before rushing to catch those horrible things, the Harare kombis that cross the road even when the robot is red. I will be the maid and student at the same time. Things are just disappearing around me. Next time, I know that one day that company car which my father used to drive will come back home again. This time with the new manager and we will have to relocate to some funny high density suburbs. I hope it won't be Mbare. Or Epworth!

If I look around me, what has really remained? From grace to grass. Isn't that a befitting description of my wretched life?

"Father. Mother. Please, talk to me. Did I vote to be your child? Did I vote for you to be my parents? God just gave you to me and me to you. I'm part of you. Tell me, what is happening around me? Around us? Where has everything gone? Why has everything gone? How has everything gone?

*****

MAN ON WHEELCHAIR

I'm all alone today. All our children are at the local high school. My wife has gone to the garden where she secretly communes with the garden soil. The two are real lovers. I could have accompanied her to that lovely place full of green vegetables but then I have no legs at all; sounds like I'm a snake? When my mother bore me, I had them both but then lost them at war. Both of them at once! That was the sacrifice I made for my people, my country; two fat legs and the blood that gushed out and flooded the battlefield. I was lucky for others lost their lives.

This July all women in the resettlement area spent hours on end in their gardens. Men are just enigmatic sometimes; they leave these poor souls to do most of the jobs alone. This year there is a lot of rapoko in Chatsworth and so the men are nearly always at "work" talking about hunting for the unending beer parties in our resettlement areas. That is the situation this July: women and their gardens; men and their parties.

Mai Ropafadzo has insisted that she wants to push me to the garden on my wheel-chair. I said no she should rest. Nearly every work on our new home calls for her attention; that is the greatest price of falling in love with a maimed war veteran. That is why I am alone at home, sitting solitarily like a lone cloud in the vast blue heavens. I don't have any regrets though for I have ample time to talk to myself, to retell stories and to create new ones all for my benefit. I have totally no misgivings if in doing so you eavesdrop and overhear the stories, for then, you and I won't forget where we are coming from, where we are and where we shall be if the sun rises again tomorrow. I retell stories so that I won't forget. Fresh wounds heal and become scars; scars remind us of yesterday's injuries. That is why I hate people who easily forget crucial issues.

My story starts with my intense love and hatred. I loved myself so much that I hated myself most. I hated myself and sacrificed my life so that tomorrow I could at least smile. I loved my parents, relatives and country so much that I ran away to join the liberation struggle. I did not bid my family and friends farewell; we just sneaked out of our dormitories and followed the comrades into the dark night. I went to war young, my right forefinger already itching to press the trigger, press it again and again until the enemy was wiped off the face of my motherland.

In my mind I could see the masses already celebrating joyfully lifting the people's banner. I could hear the people of Chipinge's triumphant shouts for then, they would stop residing on mountain tops like rock-rabbits. I could see the landless people rushing to occupy the "whiteman's" farms. I could see, hear and feel so much.

Before we had hardly crossed the eastern border, some new recruits from our home area brought the sad news: my father, sister and brother were no more. They had been shot in the heads for they had sent a son to war. Our two huts were burnt down and all beasts shot dead. The headman and the villagers were all beaten up and men's beards pulled out by the soldiers.

Blood. Sweat. Drudgery. Sorrow. Tears. Suffering. What true sweet war sacrifices? Together they watered the freedom tree for all to come and gather fruits singing, dancing and rejoicing.

"I would avenge the blood of my family members and of every murdered Zimbabwean patriot," was my new resolution. It was a shared resolution with all the other recruits. Mhondoro! The war was hotter than the oven there. There was no breathing space whatsoever. It was bang bang and boom boom nearly everywhere, every time. The enemy hunted us down from the air and horse-backs.

Then there was the infantry and the lorries deep in the bush. All the four at once hunting the guerrillas! In was in Mhondoro where I lost my dear legs and a piece of my nose for that matter. Ten comrades died during combat. Talk of the human blood and the groans of wounded and dying comrades. War is terrible: you kill or get killed. You maim others or get maimed. War is no fiction, a thriller or funny adventure.

A black Rhodesian soldier aimed his gun and shot at me. I had run short of ammunition and was vulnerable. It was comrade Chiwororo who dragged me away firing valiantly as he retreated to our mountain base. He hid me in a dark curve where I spent four days feeding on tree roots and soil. I had to drink my own urine to pacify my thirst. That was my experience. I know fellow comrades had more horrible stories to tell themselves and other people. Our children have to know them. Only the right fora should be created. We should not be too fast to blame them as being unpatriotic; they need to be empowered by giving them the right information in the right manner and from the right people.

I understand there will be a Heroesplush in Masvingo on 11 August 2006. It's a splendid idea if it is done in the right spirit. It is one way our children can be exposed to heroes of Zimbabwe. It is the right platform for them to learn about heroes and heroines through music, dance and poetry. They should know heroes are not only the comrades who died for this country but the living ones as well. They should appreciate the heroic masses who were armed with the hands, courage and patriotism but fought to the bitter end. In my view, heroes encompass all patriotic Zimbabweans minus sell-outs.

The sell-outs were and still are the proverbial witch weeds which are counter-production. Long live our political leaders. Long live all freedom fighters. Long live the masses. We are all heroes in one way or the other. The land is back and we have been resettled on areas once considered no–go-areas and meant for a minority. We now farm larger and richer tracts of land.

We travel freely. Blacks occupy key posts in government and private sector. We trade freely …the list is endless. Can there be a better reward? I suppose Rueben Barwe will be at the Heroesplush. I will be there too. The Friday train will ferry me to Masvingo where I will put up at my Uncle's in Runyararo. Suppose he bumps into me and interviews me:

"E-e Mr. Man, I understand you're a war-vet?"

"Certainly".

"What was your war name?"

"Mabhunumuchapera."

"Your real name?"

"Gore Mapuranga"

"What massage do you want to pass on to our people? Zimbabweans in general?"

"The idea of Heroesplush is wonderful for we have time to reflect on our past which bore the present. We have time to educate each other and our children, the children especially. However, because of Chimurenga 3, we now look forward to economic heroes, people who sacrifice in various ways in a bid to turn around our economy. We should shun corruption in strongest terms. Lastly, let unity, patriotism and forgiveness reign in our midst. Before anything else, first, we are all Zimbabweans …."

I could have continued with my message but Mai Ropofadzo is back from the garden and is kneeling beside me to ask after my health. I turn towards her wondering: what a wonderful and cultured creature to kneel so respectfully before a maimed war-veteran. A war-vet in his wheelchair.

*****

THE GREY HAIRED TEENAGER

In our culture, we use the forefinger to point at people and things but when he asked different people where he could find a room to rent, they pointed at the house with their protruding lips. He knew the implied message for in all their youthful years at the *dares*, did the elders not groom them into being expert problem-solvers? He recalled unlocking solutions to many riddles. So he could easily read the riddle about the house. However, what he wanted was a decent room. Just a room to rent.

The owner of the house was an old woman probably in her fifties. She was strange, at least by the way her burning eyes explored him as she spoke. When she rose to show him his room, she swung her body, occasionally looking back at him to dish out a lavish smile which loving wives would have wisely reserved for their legitimate husbands. He always responded composed. The best way to get around the current challenge was to create a gap between him and her. If he succumbed so easily to her slyness, he would be like the proverbial cockroach that was drowned in the milk it fed on.

"This is your room," she announced her right hand opening the unlocked door, the left one lightly patting on his shoulder. "Rooms to rent are like gold these days especially is Sisk. You are lucky."

He nodded studying the room but walked a step backwards from her. It's eight thousand dollars a room these days but you'll have it only for five," she said. "Five thousand dollars for everything I mean."

"Thank you mum …," he said.

"Call me Abie," she explained without a grain of shame or hesitation.

"Still a toddler at her age! Are the greying hairs decorations after all? Why doesn't she rush to the mirror and behold her rugged facial terrain? Do years move backwards?" he lamented silently. "I vow I will continue to call her 'mum' or my etiquette would have been eroded by the western culture. Call a wrinkled woman by her first name? A woman past childbearing age and the age of my real mother? Back in rural areas, at her age, she would be concerned about household chores, attending to grandchildren or cracking nuts in the sunshine. Not these filthy inclinations."

Is it the nature of the heart or the social context which negatively impact on some town people sometimes? Perhaps the setting. At Gutu Mupandawana Growth Point, he had seen crows all night around the tower-light. Day and night makes no difference. Rural crows, if ever there are any left, roost at night. They respect the night. Perhaps the setting one finds oneself matters to a great extent.

And hadn't he seen relatives saying, "Hie!" to each other as they rub shoulders in the street. He spat on his handkerchief. If this woman has been a flame whose light enticed lodgers to their death, she will be shocked," Chitauro told himself.

He knew some men were *hoto* birds which would and could not stand the force of gales. They lacked the will power to fly against the strong winds and often find themselves miles away from the place of their heart's desire.

In contrast, he would be the determined *muramba* fish which swims upwards against the flood waters that enslave the little trout, crabs and frogs. These are often washed down and bump against boulders, logs and twigs.

When he was himself again, he heard her say it again.

"This is your room. It is quite spacious and needs a married couple."

Pause.

"Are you married?"

He nodded.

Three ladies were lodgers at the house. Their rooms were further away from the landlady's bedroom. His was the nearest to the landlady's. In fact, their doors faced each other, separated by the narrow corridor. He kept his door locked and only came out when he wanted to do the dishes or use the toilet. He saw little of her but they say absence makes the heart grow fonder.

Then one day he had a chance to chat with the lady-lodgers. "You are a lucky man," they said with biting sarcasm. "If you are still single you have a sweet sixteen for yourself. At least for now, she has no child at all."

He learnt sadly that the landlady's husband had died a mysterious death when the house had just been completed. She could have killed him, the ladies alleged, for wasn't the same story being said in a number of growth points? Wasn't it rumoured that dozens of husbands were killed by their spouses upon the completion of houses? He spat onto his handkerchief again.

"You are likely to be our new landlord brother," they laughed and beat their hands together mid-air, the way gossiping women do. "She wants someone, this time not to kill, but to preserve so that she can be sustained the remaining years of her miserable years. But tough luck, there won't be a son or daughter to your name. Her womb is already withered and dead but that is not much of a bother. All she wants is a male to rule over us here, not a woman. Women are the worst enemies of their kind. They can't stay together harmoniously for a single hour. We just don't know how we were made. Study what happens at work places. One really wonders. Women can never rule as soberly and judiciously as their male counterparts," one of the ladies said.

There were more interesting observations that the male lodger noted. The spacious garden for instance was empty. No one seemed to tend it. Around the premises, there was not even a single flower, Chitauro noted too. "It's perhaps because she rents out the rooms. Lodgers perfectly know that they are accommodated for few months and evicted anytime so they often have no time for flowers and the garden. One can tell with reasonable certainty that a house has lodgers by the dull surroundings. It's just soil and grass all around."

He was lucky for he was allocated a bed where he could grow vegetables, but to his dismay, that same day she asked for a small favour. Her refrigerator was dysfunctional and wondered if he could store her meat for a day or two. He agreed but days became weeks and months .In fact, more chicken and beef came. He felt helpless.

When he wrote to his wife, Mai Joyce, to come to town, she would not stand it and maintained that the fridge was filled with the goods she had brought from the rural area and very courteously asked if the landlady could oblige her by removing her meat from the refrigerator to create more space for her goods. A woman would share anything with other women not her husband and special electrical gadgets. Not Mai Joyce.

The next morning, Chitauro's vegetable bed had been dug up overnight, the water and electric bills and the rent had quadrupled. He simply looked at his wife and sighed. *****

THE WRESTLERS

Two agile wrestlers sprang into the empty ring and the starting bell rang. The rather lean figure by some inexplicable maneuvering, pinned the hulk of a man, his wrangler, down on the ground and the winning bell rang. Spontaneous shouts of horror and disbelief echoed deafeningly throughout the congested stadium. Involuntarily, MaTrouble had found herself joining in the frenzy. That match marked the end of the programme and this lone fan stirred and lazily extricated herself from the caressing comfort of her pink velvet sofas and switched off the television.

"Whew!" she sighed holding the back part of her head with both palms. Trouble already in the first grade at a multi-racial school discontinued his haphazard scribbling on numerous white papers strewn all around him, studied her and then with pencil in hand asked, "What's it mom?"

"Nothing."

"You, bored?"

"No, Trouble."

"Who won?"

"Not sure about the wrestlers' names but the lean man beat the huge man. It was so surprising."

"You enjoyed it then?"

"A bit."

"Does the pastor like merciless kids? Or Dads or Moms?

"No", she answered suspiciously.

"And father, does he want to be a wrestler? He doesn't go to church. He calls the beer hall his church. Does he want to be cruel like Hoggan and the British Bull Dog?"

"Your dad is a good man Tee. One day he will go to church."

This was a sour prelude to her plan. Here was innocence speaking prophetically inducing guilty within her heart. Wasn't it true that she was waiting eagerly but feverishly for the first battle with him? The very moment he stepped into the lounge, she would stand for her rights. A woman would turn into a victor.

She knew he was unsuspecting and oblivious of this new feeling that kept knocking at her heart. Many times she had suppressed it but a stubborn stump, its shoots had always appeared.

To occupy trouble, she fished a cold coke from the fridge, opened and gave it to him. She needed a free chance to rehearse all her plans for anytime from now he could appear from work. But how would Tee feel if he witnessed the first live wrestling show between his parents? In fact, wrestle for what? Money? Popularity? Title? Power? Theirs would be a wrestle because they both had fat sums and would not reach a consensus on whose money should be used where and for what?

"So your problem is the presence of money?" a voice asked.

"No", she responded.

"So..? "All this long he has taken advantage of me just because am a woman. Just because I go to church, he thinks he can bully me around like that. Just because ...Can't stomach that anymore. He squanders all his pay every month then invites me how to budget how my salary can be used. Every month for the five years we have been married. He boozes every created day amidst stout diseased bitches.

'Rarely does he buy any groceries or clothes for trouble or me. He just wrestles to win recognition in every beer hall around Harare. Just a name. Just that and he develops feathers. He forgets we have a family, this child, fees and bills to pay every month. His monies are leisure monies and my salary born out of sweat should be budgeted for. I've been tolerant this far and this is the farthest I can go. If he could have turned over a new leaf, five years should have been ample time to do that, she complained".

Ma Trouble refused to accept that tolerance and meekness were power under control. Not now. The unchanging, ever worsening brute had fought many winning battles against her and had been the unchallenged victor all this long. This day would herald a new era when he should turn the victor-victim.

Mai Trouble paced up and down the vast lounge ready to charge and pounce. She cast her itching red eyes at the familiar wall hanging and the words: "CHRIST IS THE HEAD OF THIS FAMILY," greeted her. This she took away and hid away. Next she removed the picture frame full of both John, herself and Tee. This too she hid away. To complete the programme, the cross should disappear too but when she extended her right arm, her heart thudded. Just then, Ba Tatenda came in.

Little Tatenda shot towards his father shrieking with excitement. The man of the house then proceeded to sit close to his wife. He waited painfully for her greetings; the usual cheerful, wively greetings. They were not forthcoming. The storm was brewing and when Baba Tatenda proceeded to serve himself with food and water, the fiery fire was ready to scorch and consume anything found along its path. Trouble should have sensed this tenseness.

"Dad, you and mom don't smile at each other today like the wrestlers?" Trouble broke the silence.

Two pairs of eyes shot silently at each other. That very night when trouble slept in his separate room, he could hear loud threatening voices and painful cries. Then there were these queer sounds as if something was being smashed.

The next morning, Ma Trouble saw little Trouble's poem perched on the coffee table.

"I don't like wrestling,

I don't like mom

And dad

Because they like wrestling,

And are wrestlers.

I love smiling pictures."

*****

FIRST CLASS WITCHES

A weird nocturnal dr-r-r shakes me from my deep sweet sleep. Its echoes last a few terrible seconds so, I at least console myself that the sound will not recur. Before I can fully recover from my initial shock, the awe-striking, earth-shaking, reverberation comes again like an unwelcome visitor. Everything quakes: all doors bang against their frames. The windows clatter and squeak. My bed dance clumsily and I dance on the dancing bed. It appears the walls can curve in at any time and it's not surprising that in a few seconds' time I can be part of the rubble. I freeze. "Witchcraft of the highest order," I conclude.

To hell with the Witchcraft Suppression Act, I condemn. If this is not witchcraft what else can it be? Forty years of my life. I haven't experienced such a phenomena. Our fathers too. I begin to wonder if some of our legislators have been born and bred on Mars. We have grown up being told that in Chipinge witchcraft is a brisk business. They sell dried crocodile bile which they use to poison each other at drinking parties. In Chiredzi, its lightning. Zaka, too, is well known for its best witches. So why do all these parliamentarians come up with all these funny pieces of legislature? You call a true witch, a witch and you get into trouble with the law. Incredible! I am yet to challenge the Act today, at dawn.

My palpitating heart has steadied somehow. So I grope for a match-box and on lighting the candle, I discover that it is around 12:30am on 23 February 2006. The violent quaking should have occurred at around 12:20am, therefore. This is the witch's hour. Ask any Zimbabwean he knows it's the evil hour.

Frankly speaking, I have never seen witches myself but have heard several stories about them. I have also met them in my dreams where they pursued me riding on fast hyenas. Somehow, I mysteriously developed wings and always fly away to safety.

I can't resist this urge; the urge to expose them, I will shout out their names for the whole new resettlement area to know them. We came to settle on the AI farms to farm crops not this witchcraft. Shameless beings.

Today, I will expose them. The best place will be on top of the tall anti-hill at the edge of my yard. That place is strategic even for beer criers who invite people for "seven days"– the traditional brew. It is even the best place if your husband beats you up and you want to retaliate by pouring out grotesque secrets everyone should not know. The ant-hill will be the right place. Now let me rehearse what I will say out:

"I have experienced the quake your ghosts have caused at my zinc house at night but I want you to know that even if my husband has been away from home, you have utterly failed to destroy me.

'I know you all: your leader is Mai Tendai. The vice is Magumbo. I know that young group comprises eight women and one male. You hate me for beating you at farming and for the zinc house we built. You all still dwell in pole and dagga structures in this century! Shame on you. Who doesn't know that you're jealous of my husband who is a headmaster? I have the ten suits because I am the wife of the headmaster? I have ten suits because I am the wife of the headmaster who happens to be one of the best farmers in this resettlement area.

"And you, Mai Dzoro, you have decided to eat people's livers so that you can grow stout like Mai Tendai? You think if you remain slim the whirlwinds will carry you away or your husband will send you back to your parents' home? I bet you, you will not eat my liver. Not mine, come rain come thunder."

This will be part of my message. I will broadcast it to the entire village and afterwards, I will account for my words. I am very prepared to stand in the box and defend myself in court. Witches are as real as life and death.

Funny, dawn comes quickly and it's time for me to strike the iron while it is still hot. I roll out of the bed in my night dress, unlock the door but there is this silhouette of a female figure. My heart thumps. I step backwards into the room and bang the door. Someone laughs outside.

"What a coward you are MaMoyo. It's already dawn. Come out, I have a word with you." I know the owner of the voice. It is Madhuve, my neighbour. I fret a bit because we normally don't visit each other at such an odd time. I go out laughing at my cowardice. We both laugh.

"Did you sleep well with all the quaking that has taken place MaMoyo? The world is ending as the Bible has foretold," Madhuve starts. "You experienced the quake too?" I sat startled. "The whole of Zimbabwe should have been shaken," she explains.

Guilt preys on me. What I had thought was a quake restricted to my house should have affected many people country-wide. In my heart, I secretly thank God for Madhuve's timely arrival before I have made one of the greatest blunders in my life. Good neighbourliness is like the sweet scent that attracts bees.

***** 2006****

THE MADE CHASE

That was perhaps improper but indeed typical of Ganyani. He planned his things secretly and long enough but when he had ultimately made rehearsals and made a resolution, he stuck to it like a leech. At this point, he would be impervious to any form of advice from anyone, not even his spouse. Anyone who dared block his already cleared broad highway risked being run over. Mai Dzikamai, his wife, knew him well but surprisingly, when Ganyani broke the news of his latest decision, she was baffled and felt helpless. All she could say after recovering from the shock was: "But Ganyani, how could you plan such a crucial undertaking solo…?"

The man of the house looked hard into her eyes and grunted, "I could have briefed you about it, but as mere formality. Everything is in place now and I will fly next week. I'm U.K bound."

He was going to U.K willy-nilly but there was one disturbing phenomenon: it was the horrible, haunting dream. The last week before his departure, it had kept knocking at his door in its characteristic poetic tones:

This chase you've begun

Is a senseless and futile one

For many a man and woman I know

Were with serpent craftiness

Enticed from the comfort of their mansions

And brimming family bliss

To pursue passing winds

Which no mortal hand has ever

Nor can ever grip.

Some hungers, some thirsts, are insatiable

Only the fool is full of these

To run after the rushing wind is madness

I say its utter madness.

However, the poet remained anonymous. Were they ancestors or some form of divine advice? What was the 'chase,' 'the wind,' 'the hunger' and what not? In fact, how did all these relate to him or his imminent departure? Somehow, though vaguely, he knew the poem was highly connotative for hadn't he done Literature at A-level? But wasn't a belief in a mere dream some mild form of superstition? Believing in a dream? Wasn't it ridiculous for an educated professional to have some form of belief in a dream? Surely, anyone capable of sleeping could dream as well, but try as he could, the more he tried to bury the dream in a bottomless pit of forgetfulness, the louder it came, but, had all those who knew him nick-named him "storm" for nothing? A storm tears and forcibly creates a way where there was previously none. Most things in its way bow or crumble to rubble as it uncompromisingly bulldozes its way.

The London he was so mad about didn't give him any peace of mind. First, with stubbornness and persistence of an avenging spirit, the wretched dream always revisited him. Second, were his father's words? He saw the advice in a new way. "Those were witty, prophetic, simple yet complex words that I should have taken heed of," he said looking vacantly and sickly at the white ceiling of his room.

Hadn't he scorned, shunned the advice freely flowing from the old man's heart? By the way, how did the words go?

"My son, I don't speak to convince you but to advice you. I know you too well for I natured you. No man can make the owl change its tunes that is why owls have ever been hooting. That is why they will continue to hoot in future. Likewise, the dove will coo forever. You are what we know you are, have been and would be. I speak these humble words so that when the snare catches with you and you are in dire danger, at least, you would look back and say: "Had I known! Had I cherished the advice! Had I listened!

"Know this my son, London is a name. It's a place on earth, not in heaven. It has its beauties and flaws like any other place you know. It's not an ideal place for either a married man or woman to go alone without one's spouse. If Mai Dzikamai and you were flying together, my words would be unfounded. If you 'burn' when you are thousand miles apart who would pacify those hard-to bridle emotions? The opposite is true of Mai Dzikamai. The result is infidelity. So know it my child, though you have read books. I've read from life experience's books. You have started setting a lethal time bomb that would explode and blast your once happy marriage. The perpetual tears on your wife's cheeks don't augur well for you. I fear for you.

"And your boy child, Dzikamai! He needs both parents around. A child shouldn't be like the broiler chicks you rear for slaughter. I learnt sadly that machines hatch them. That poor thing, the chick, grows up not knowing the hen, its mother." Children should not be like your television that can be remotely controlled. Well-groomed citizens begin at family level; spoil the foundation and build a frail, shameful house that can be a death-trap to the inmates. Rearing a child should be a concerted effort of both parents first. The wider community comes second. But how many children take up all these queer cultures from some of the uncultured maids? It's a disgrace. It's a shame. Maids can never be equal substitutes for parents.

"Remember too, my son, that you have a profession, some business projects here in Gonye village and in Gutu Mupandawana

Growth Point. You have two mansions, one in this village and the other in the growth point. You have a car that is envied by many. You were blessed with a faithful and industrious wife who, once in a while visits South Africa to import electrical gadgets and sundry other goods. You still have the "whiteman's" dishes on your table in spite of the economic hardships faced by the nation. What then could have inspired you to shun home? We know abject poverty drives some from their homes. For you it's the opposite. This I will tell my son, the sea will never get filled with water, neither will the ground. That is why rich and influential people in our society go on to steal even if their pillows and mattresses are stuffed with crisp dollar notes. By our very nature, we can never stop yearning but we should at times train ourselves to be self-satisfied with just enough. There is a certain longing and dissatisfaction that is healthy for a man but if it is tantamount to greed, such longing, such hunger or thirst, is misguided and destructive. And lastly, pounds can never replace you. We are nearly graves now. Money, pounds, can't see, hear, walk or talk for us. I know, I can't change you…..Go in peace."

It was the longest speech ever delivered by the old man at his *dare*-men's meeting place. As he took stock of his life, one year after leaving home, how much have come to pass? Didn't guilt torture him when Mai Dzikamai talked to him on the line? Didn't the phrase "my darling" that she used often on the line torment him more? At the same words, didn't he wish she was close by so that he could draw her close to him and kiss her? He longed to hug her the way he did when he reported back from work or journey. Alas, they were worlds apart and that was why the once victor of the past few months had become a victim. He was now the victor-victim.

"Because this has happened to me, perhaps she too….! Women who visit other countries can do it especially when they are desperate for anything," Ganyani fretted. "No woman can be stronger than a man in this area," he added.

In fact, what had made him leave home in the first place? Wasn't it his pride, his conceit? Flying overseas to create a name, to remain conspicuous in society, to stick out and outshine anyone else in the six villages; Gonye, Moto, Magara, Mukiyo, Guramatunhu and

Chivasa. That was the secret behind everything he had done at home; doing things to prove he could do it better than anyone else and get all the attention. Wasn't he the first one out of the six neighbouring villages to visit the African London, South America's capital city? When every Jack and Jill began to visit the same destination, that was when he was wounded at heart and thought of the whiteman's London. He had to change his usual destination.

No-one should however, point an accusing finger at him, he felt. Who in the vast world wasn't in one way or the other glory-seeking? Self-seeking? He thought of the young beauty pageants.

"Damn them! They are worse for they strut on the stages half-naked (being legitimately sexually abused by rich adult men) all to get recognition. To get a name on the map of beauty queens. Who indeed could be spotless when it came to this subject?" Ganyani consoled himself.

Housewives were not spared either for some of them clog displays and kitchen units with eye-catching and fanciful utensils that are never used by family members but are there to be admired by visitors. The housewives always get a share of that praise or admiration. So, he always consoled himself that he was not alone in this madness, vanity.

Everyone at home was talking about him. His family was secretly proud that one of their family members was jostling with long-based Britons and speaking in their mother-tongue. He was enthused by that realisation but somehow some mild form of nostalgia was slowly but surely creeping into him but he told himself that he would die in London and be FLOWN home in a LONDON CASKET. With this strange illness, who knew, this could happen sooner or later. He desperately wanted pounds to be littered around his corpse so that even in death, the people would wonder at him. He wished the mourners would say it loud and clear: "WE'VE NEVER SEEN SUCH A CASKET BEFORE. HE WAS IN LONDON EARNED POUNDS, DIED IN LONDON AND WAS FLOWN BACK HOME.

At that moment, Shirley's poem "Death the Leveller" rang in his mind. He was deeply hurt. Very hurt indeed.

*****2003*****

94

TWICE A MOTHER

When the old lady, Mbuya Nyikadzino, looked back into the distant past, one would have concurred with her that it once rained on her. However, the events of the past five years had heralded a new twist and it had indeed poured on her. It was calamity after calamity in her family. Every speaker at the burial of her third and last son, Tinos, echoed similar sentiments: the angels of death had come to camp at her home. Naturally, people expected that she would shed oceans of bitter tears at the latest tragic event. She didn't. She just couldn't. So, her withered cheeks remained dry even when wailing village women came hurling themselves onto her fail pair of bony legs. Her response was a deep groan whose millions of teardrops were real yet invisible. This was queer and some people began to raise eyebrows.

"She should be worse than a witch. Witches who kill their own blood would at least shed crocodile tears in order to cover up for their fiendish nature. Surely, she had experienced three deaths within such space of time but do our wells of tears dry up? Aren't they perennial springs that only dry at death? The old lady should be that proverbial hen that cracks its own eggs to feed on them," secret gossips speculated.

It was apparent there was no consensus. Could a witch be so relentless as to wipe out three souls within five years? All because she has a demoniac and insatiable appetite for human meat? True indeed, witches were said to exist but they would not kill so unwisely; so indiscriminately as to make it clear to the world that they were the culprits. Furthermore, wasn't it known that the witches rationalised before bewitching anyone. If then the old lady got rid of all the breadwinners to pave way for abject poverty and the crushing burden of having to look after five miserable grandchildren, would that make any sense at the old lady's twilight age? In fact, wasn't there a popular village story told of two witches who disagreed on whether to kill a local woman or not, all because the would-be victim lavishly provided free milk to one of the witches? If the benevolent woman would disappear from the face of the earth, it would be a hard to blow to the beneficiary. So the witches would not agree and they spent the entire night arguing. The prospective woman was eventually spared. So even if the old lady would have been a witch, such slaughter would have been untenable.

It was Zvingobe, the most outspoken villager, who chided the gossips. "Our people have become *Tsikamutandas*, typical witch-hunters. This old lady's eyes are dead and can hardly see. She can't hunt for roots in the forests anymore. Her ears, her body are dying and one can't expect her to ride a rushing hyena successfully. She would fall and maim himself for life. Let's call a spade a spade; the witch is this global 'stranger' that threatens to annihilate humankind. Those in our society with white collar jobs and have fat monies to squander, often get victimised. So, leave the old lady alone".

A number of mourners secretly eyed each other and nodded again and again. No one would dare say what Zvingobe said for they feared to say the truth, for the people say the truth hurts. If ever they would discuss the subject, it would be in a manner that impressed the hearers' ears. Wasn't it a cultural canker? Doing things to please, to cover up weaknesses? In the Shona culture, for instance, if a couple which fights every created day gets a visitor for some days, it would strive to be the most peaceful and loving couple in the world. Even naughty children will be eyed secretly if they start doing anything out of place. All grotesque tendencies are slid under the carpet so that the visitor sees only the roses and go away talking about their host.

The time for selected speakers arrived. It was the most horrible time for the old lady. "The family members would say out the shameful lies again. They will pledge to help and stand by me through thick and thin but when the people have dispersed they disappear for good...." Indeed, when one extended family member rose to address the mourners they clapped hands for him. He pledged to ease Mbuya Nyikadzino's burden by sending in "substantial" help at the end of each month. All the orphans will be sent to school and their education paid for. The old lady just looked away vacantly.

It was the chief's address that brought her back to reality. She revered him for she said he spoke sense and was down-to-earth in all his dealings.

"My sincere and deepest sorrow goes to the Tichafa family and especially to the old lady whose joy has been stolen again by such misfortune. My heart bleeds when our very future, our breadwinners, the tenderest of my people are stumped daily in our sight leaving behind them legions of young and helpless orphans who have to be fended for by skeletons like us. It hurts us. It hurts me. The bloodthirsty axe is on the necks of those who should support and bury us. At our age, can we dig graves and bury each other? We are fearful of the days when grey-haired octogenarians would spent days digging a single grave to bury their dead. Such days are imminent and insight. It will be a grim state of things indeed."

Then the chief asked the old lady to rise. She groped around for the walking stick taking ages to find it and at last battled to assume stooping position, careful to keep balancing on the stick. Even then, her whole frame shook, her lifeless eyes dully looking at no-one in particular.

"You have all eyes to see," the chief resumed. "At such age, the old lady is a child again but the present challenges dictates that she be a mother again. Twice a mother in a life-time is too burdensome a responsibility. The logical thing would have been that she be well looked after. That she rests after the labour of bringing up a family."

The chief went further to ask the orphans to rise for the mourners to see. They mourners shook their heads as if on cue. Everyone wondered where the old lady would start from and how? All her late sons had not left behind huts, goats, sheep or cattle. They always thought there was no need of rushing to do things but people say procrastination is the thief of time. They had died planning. At the end of the long speech, the chief underscored the need for their working sons to throw up structures at their rural home. Towns were not real homes, he had said. To the old lady's relief too, the chief pledged he would see her benefitting from the recently adopted Zunde raMambo project.

When the people had buried the deceased and fed, they began to disperse in groups. The old lady fretted and wanted to re-gather them. She wanted them to solace her, to give her reassurance that they would always stand by her until her last day.

"A mother again at such sunset!" she pronounced to herself as she nibbled at the cooking sadza she had been offered.

*****

WHEN THE MAID STRIKES

Tamburai had heard her employees say it repeatedly and it was then that she wondered if, given the present situation, she could not rightly utter the same words: "I am tired of working for peanuts." Indeed within one year, they had successfully gone on strike more than once and their salaries had been hiked. When the new salary packages were publicised, Mr and Mrs Mbizvo went wild with joy and hugged each other in celebration.

Then Tamburai heard the two say it for the first time; "The only language the employer would not ignore is the language of industrial action. It is a shame that they deliberately wait for things to worsen and then react." Those were their words. She began to feel those were her words too—words that had remained silent within her but wanted to be heard and digested by her employers.

That tendency to remain mum when the urge to speak out was irresistible was very much against the advice her late mother had imparted to her. She had said, "Sad and dark thoughts are thorns that prick the heart. The heart, my daughter, is a fragile egg. If one allows boiling thoughts to hatch and breed unchecked, it will explode without further warning. The heart should be flushed at intervals. When you speak out, you flush it and avoid unnecessary crises."

Those were the wise words of the loving mother who now lay several feet under the ground. Tamburai convinced herself, however, that verbal words were not the only vehicles of communication. Actions were perhaps more effective and spoke even louder. Accordingly, she started to wake up earlier than ever, cleaned the mansion more thoroughly than before and showed a higher degree of diligence and responsibility than ever.

There was neither compliment nor any pay rise from her employers. She wondered why. It was then that she left every piece of work half-done. She wanted them to complain but all the madam said was, "If you are tired of us leave us alone and return to the wretched rural area where we saved you from the burning wrath of your stepmother and stinking poverty."

She had remained silent about the issue of her wages. She had fumed and reminded her that they were her saviours from the hell at her home, that she was an ungrateful traveller, who through actions cursed the cave that had sheltered her from a deluge of rainfall. She indeed, should be a grateful worshipper who serve her masters faithfully in all weather.

At times Tambu would cry pitifully and longed her mother was alive. Her father too. What mercy could she expect from a stepmother? Did she care if she was hungry, sad, thirst or...? Who in the vast world did not know the kind of hearts that resided in most step mothers? And what did her step mother say when she left Wazvaremhaka?

"Go with the Mbizvos to town. They are our relatives but you are not going to eat, belch and sleep. You are going to work. If you grow tired of them you should come back home. I need someone to help around the place since I am always alone here. When you go to Harare, remember us too. We need soap, cooking oil and salt." The year was nearly over now and indeed, she had sent one grocery item or the other without fail. In fact, she nearly always used up to $8 000.00 she earned for that purpose. It meant she had little or nothing left to buy clothes and shoe wear.

All the three dresses she had were donations she had received from the madam, a little bit torn and faded though. But these were donations not her pay. Surely, her employers had had two pay rises within a year because they did not want to work "for peanuts."

Facts are stubborn; at the end of the day it was all very clear she had come to Harare to benefit others more. The gains she had were exclusively three: free food, accommodation and a lighter skin that had been tamed by treated water. For all the services she offered all days along?

She resolved to complain formally to her mistress, "Would you oblige me by reviewing my pay? I think I can hardly meet my needs."

"Who in the world gets enough? Who can you say is really satisfied? Go back to the rural area if you want. We give you everything here-free food, water, accommodation, clothes and in return you complain like that." Tambu suddenly developed a new urge. She wanted to jump at the madam's neck and strangle her to death. She shook with anger. Grotesque retaliatory plans began to slowly colonise her mind and showcase themselves before her mind's eye.

She embraced them all without discarding any. She began spitting into the couple's breakfast, lunch and supper and watched them eat everything. She observed all this with demoniac glee. At that moment, she felt something lift from her burdened heart. She was relieved.

As if goaded by fiendish forces, she would at times switch on all the electrical appliances for a considerable length of time. She would dash out and ululate quietly as the meter raced by. She grinned. Though the Mbizvos had proved as stingy as *chapungus*-the eagles which will not allow their feathers pluck off and float in the skies – they would pay hefty bills to ZESA. That would serve them right, she reasoned.

She grinned as she reviewed all the tactics lined up to fix the couple: a bit of urine in their mazoe; using their toothbrushes to clean the chamber; a bit of sputum in their stew. She was happy but hurt and prayed that she had a way of making them aware she was punishing them but at the same time shuddered at the thought of what her fate would be if they knew about it.

*****

THE COUNTRY BOY

The horn of his Toyota Cressida blared irritatingly, playing havoc with the rather tranquil village morning hours, prematurely awakening late sleepers, among them some of the worst village drunkards.

To get full results, he lowered all the windows of his car and the once confined deafening sounds from Simon Chimbetu's new release riotously exploded out and rippled over the villages nearby along the Gutu-Basera road. The response was tremendous for, like *ishwa* – the edible ants attracted to a bright source of light, the adventurous youths, for want of cheap, unpaid for entertainment, stampeded out of smouldering, grass-thatched huts and male quarters to intercept the music car that travelled at a leisurely speed.

At last, the awaited car would arrive, the sweet lyrics adorning the rather dull atmosphere, a lazy cloud of dust billowing behind in eternal pursuit. "Oh! It's Dadirai. The boy from the village next to ours. The boy we learnt with at Midzi High a couple of years ago. Fortune has knocked on his doors ultimately. He was a loafer in spite of his distinctions," said one.

"In Zimbabwe, no connections, no career opportunities. You have to connect with big fish to of influence," responded the other. "Surely, these days, success depends on who you know and what you can offer… not your very good passes…." On and on they talked like untiring chattering monkeys.

Dadirai was generous. He waved at them all, at times calling them by their first names or nicknames. This was now very familiar ground where he had herded cattle, sheep, goats and notoriously stubborn male donkeys that ran away kilometres in pursuit of females on heat. This was the area where they fought in the valleys to get titles. This was the area whose rivers they swam in playing their favourite water game *Hero sadzamukuche*. Had they clearly seen him, Dadirai Zunde; the loafer who had passed his 'O' Level with distinctions but still roamed about the village like a lost spirit?

In the rear view mirror, Dadirai caught a glimpse of the mob retreating in the settling dust. Somehow he could tell that he was the subject of discussion and instantly, he felt like a king. Everything, everyone appeared so base, so minute, and so inconspicuous. It was incredible that some powers, divine or ancestral, had miraculously raised him from the dust to sit among kings.

"Never have I been so generous, so patriotic, splashing music, broadcasting it everywhere! To sullen and quiet hills and mountains. To sunbathing rock rabbits and folks who brood over morning fires, unentertained," he mused.

At Gonye Township, he indicated and turned right. Even here there were people, dancing, though fewer than he had experienced before. The faces were now very familiar. This morning, some of them danced wildly under the influence of the previous day's borrowed beer. Some waved to stop the car and Dadirai had to switch off the engine. More music fanatics poured onto the scene like flies upon carrion. They danced, indifferent to who their DJ was. They minded the music, not the driver. Glued to his seat, Dadirai joined in the frenzy of excitement. He would nod, eyes deliberately half open, then swerve to the right and to the left. Only when the car was pulling off did the youths realise that it was their locally educated boy. They waved to stop him and he waved back but kept on travelling about a kilometre due south. To appear modest, he turned down the volume and reduced speed. A thud! Another! It was his heart palpitating with joy.

"Soon I will see them all. My parents, relatives, neighbours. Some will die of envy while others will be on seventh heaven. Do they know that I bought this? Minister's car. Do they know also that I will marry and wed soon? This is September. Come December, there will be a white wedding. I say to you my parents, rest from your labours. Wipe away all your tears and sweat. Your gaping kraals shall henceforth breathe with livestock again. No more grass thatched huts. We've to burn them down for I have real money in my pockets and in the bank. No more candle-lit rooms. No more *maputi* or roasted groundnuts for breakfast."

Dadirai thought of what he would say. His car stopped beside the thorn strewn gate. When he hooted, six perplexed faces peeped from the kitchen door in turns. "We have no one with a car in our clan. Who can that be?" the eyes seemed to say.

It was his father, in his characteristic baggy, old overalls, with patch upon patch, on bare calloused feet who advanced towards the waiting car, fearful and curious. Dadirai resolved to come out of the car. "Ah, do I see well? Is this really my blood?" his father said as he started running towards him. Dadirai hugged him again and again. "I'm, father. Your flesh and blood," he pronounced tears of joy cascading down his cheeks. Then the yells and hammering of feet.

"Dadi! Dadi!" voices of different pitches chorused the venerable name. Dadirai shook hands with his mother, his two brothers; Runo and Tavonga, his sister Porai and lastly grandpa, Tongoona who had tottered last chanting a hymn to the ancestors.

Dadirai woke up weakly and reached for his beer-stained blue jeans torn to shreds on the knees and with a distinct black square patch on the back. Contemplatively, slowly, he fitted his thin frame into it. That done, he threw on his f added black T-shirt without any further scrutiny. From behind the wooden mortar (which he used at night as a security device) he retrieved two home-made car tyre sandals, slid his wide, cracked feet in and then pushed the squeaking door open. After spying and satisfying himself that no-one was watching, he stole out of the hut. Cocking his ears, a safe distance away, the usual sharp scratch of a metal spoon on a clay pan greeted him. "Preparing *maputi* for breakfast? No ways," he told himself.

He then hastened his pace towards the crudely built Blair toilet, passed by it, skipped the crumbling wire fence and came to the empty kraal where scores of healthy cattle once huddled in their tens. In their stead, where flourishing wild rapoko grass and black beetles engaged in a funny chase. A heart sore.

"My parents sowed healthy certified seeds; they reaped the howling mad wind. They invested in a successful failure – a loafer with worthless good passes that mean nothing ...."

He could not face his parents. He was a source of pain and disappointment, not because he had failed them in any way or had they failed him. No! It was the system somewhere,

113

someone where no ordinary hands could access.

Just, then a beer crier's voice could be heard in the distance, "*Ngome kumo!* – Beer party at Mr Nhumbu's today. Bring along your blankets and pillows for you won't be able to stagger back home. It's super, super opaque beer from pure finger millet and brewed the very olden way. The early bird catches the worm, the late ones will find empty beer pots."

Dadirai began to walk, kicking stones and stumps. In no time, he was facing the sign post of his former secondary school. The words, "EDUCATION FOR A BETTER LIFE" stood out quite visibly. Without wasting any time, he collected a handful of sand. Furiously, he sent it flying onto the unhearing, unfeeling, and unseeing structure, spitting and cursing all the time.

*****

THE UNFAIR PENALTY

The nurse turns towards her, clutching heaps of pills. She hands them over to her and the patient, with dull, lifeless eyes peeping from her deep dark sockets, grudgingly extends her emaciated arms to accept them.

"All this my child?" she ventures to say.

"Yes, mum," the nurse says.

"But you have never given me such heaps before, not for the past weeks I've been here. That's why I've asked my daughter."

"You are quite right mum. This time you will need lots of them. You are being discharged today, this morning, you know? It will prove expensive if you will have to board a bus to collect pills from here. All the way from Honde Valley?"

"So, I'm going home? Today? This morning?"

The nurse remains silent. She deliberately starts fidgeting with boxes and containers strewn on the table. The patient just sits on the bench and never stands to go.

115

"How can that be my daughter? I'm still unwell. You discharge such skeletous these days? Such bones! Rattling bones! Our youthful days, they discharged recovered people. If you inject me this once, I think I'll be O.K. Pills always refuse me. But since I came over here, I have had these pills."

"Don't worry, you can always come back. Meantime, the hospital has decided that you ...."

"I'm old my child and can read between the lines. The hospital? It's you who have decided. Is the hospital a person? You doctors and nurses! You decided to send me away. You think I'm a nuisance. An eyesore." Silence, then, "Alright, I will go. I may as well bid you all farewell for now and forever for we may never meet again ...."

Wells of tears form quickly as she arises. The nurses look away. She hears the door open. Then the faint patter of feet. The sound soon disappears. She sighs as she waits for the next patient to come in. "Oh, what face? A page full of horror. I can't face that," she says relieved.

Back in the female ward, the patient takes ages to pack her belongings. She mutters to herself each time. Looking around in the female ward, she discovers that her other mate lay still in their beds, awake though.

"See you again if we will, friends. I've been discharged. Thanks for sharing our common plight with me," she pronounces.

In their beds, the mates roll to one side, painstakingly, sickly, and face their mate open-mouthed, groaning the more. A few better ones just looked at each other and shook their heads sadly.

Her bag slung on one shoulder, she drags herself towards the hospital gate. Instinctively, she discovers she is being attacked! Eyes! A sea of eyes is scanning her, railing accusations. The security guard at the gate too. She picks up the message.

"Oh, no!" she fires back at the eyes. "Why should you always hasten to make conclusions? Hear it from me for I have a story to tell.

When I got married in 1965, I was a virgin. Full virgin! Unadulterated. If my late husband were here, he would have confirmed this. He is the sole man ever to see my thighs and to explore them. Tichafa Pindo knows this, late as he is. He knows that till his miserable death, I have not parted with even a grain of my love. It was all for one man. All of it pure and brimming. Even until this hour, no man has ever known me. Sharing my love? That is dog-shit to me. A non-starter. So why do these eyes shoot undeservedly at me?

What I know for certain is that I did not drag the snake into our marriage. Perhaps it was him, a razor-blade or ----! God knows. But if it was him ----! Tichafa, did I ever refuse you on the bed old as I was? Other women of my age do but on my part, my fire was still alive, my love undying. Was there a good reason to wonder away from me? Women are women. They are flesh and blood. Temporal! Temporary too on this earth. There are no women of stone, gold or silver. Only the fanciful mind can create such ones.

Oh this lethal creature! How it eats away ravenously at my nerves. How it sucks all life out of the body. Death of a family. That it is."

She arrives at the bus stop so clogged with people chatting and laughing. She is startled.

"Are there people who can still crack jokes and laugh? Jokes. Laughs. Life. Health."

Then without prior warning, what she has feared all along begins to happen. Loud, incessant rumbles begin to roar. It's her stomach. Imminent shame. A discomfiture. She looks around with apprehension. "There is no toilet around," she laments. If it were in the rural areas, I would have crouched behind a bush."

Should she revisit the hospital toilets? With her sore, swollen legs, she would help herself on the way. The toilets appear miles away. Looking around, she picks out a suburban house just a stone's throw from the bus stop. Her fear melts away as she totters towards it.

As she enters the unlocked gate unannounced, she reflects. "It's one of the greatest shames an adult can experience. Messing oneself in public like some of the worst drunkards I know. Chiripo, for instance. I wonder how he manages to meet eyes with his children, wife and neighbours the following day. He is that I —do-not-care-what-you-think type of a person. He is the type that won't care even if the sun rises in the west and sets in the east. Young ones should never ever see an adult's stools. It's a taboo. Deplorable!"

Climbing the two steps proves a typical uphill climb. However, at last, she is successful. Feebly, anxiously, she knocks on the glass door. There is a patter of feet inside and a minute later, horrified faces invade her through the spotlessly clean dining room window. "Can I use your toilet?" she begs clapping slightly. The eyes look at each other and then back at her. "Please!" she pleads.

An elderly woman opens the window rather too emotionally. "This is town," she says seriously and immediately shuts the window, rather harshly shattering into pieces in the process. Too late to mend. The buzzing flies confirm it. She creeps sheepishly away something watery and stinking racing down her thin shrivelled thighs.

"This is town. Where can I clean this? This is town. Do towns not have people have ailing relatives? This is town. Now I know.

Town people have no hearts anymore. No emotions. No love for outsiders. They can't share anything with a stranger! Towns! Town people! Town life! Fast life!

Just then a mini-bus stops at the bus stop. Forgetting her latest predicament, she fishes a quilt from her slinging bag, ties it around her thin waist and surprisingly, frantically waves for the bus to stop. On arrival, she fights to lift her first leg but before she manages to do so, the sniffing conductor roughly shovels her aside. "She is mad. Smells of something. Start the engine driver." "No, my child but ----," she attempts to explain in vain.

Soon, the loaded bus groans away exuding black, black smoke that engulfs her. When it clears, she is all alone. Dejected. Rejected.

***** *Written before ARVs were in use by many AIDS patients in 2000 Zimbabwe*****

TIME BOMB

I've tirelessly confronted legions of woes and wars all this long but have never raised my feeble hands in surrender though at times I feel I am being crushed like the doomed dry millet under the grinding stone. At least, as I can remember, I've always emerged triumphant, strengthened and more resolute. That's it, the naked truth. Yet, I'm not in a position to fully explain why but one of these days perhaps the truth will ultimately dawn on me and the veil will be broken to shreds.

One reason can be the fact that while adversities tend to weaken many people, they seem to impact differently on me for, when they have hit and gone, I become hardened. Towering mountains become valleys and the rugged, jagged terrain flat lands. I'm like the concrete that gets hardened at the presence of water, not that cheap stuff that crumbles to shambles at the presence of water. Then, there is this stubbornness in me that defy defections. Once I've set my mind on doing, something. I shun any wavering but like the archer's unmissing arrow, I dart for the target...That's me --- at least what I think I am.

Four babies! All from this withered womb! Do they not adorn the wet river banks where some ancient village women secretly laid them to rest? Do they not lie that the deep sleep in the earth's dark womb? All after those maddening pangs of child- birth pains!

No pretense here, for I am a mother; grief gnawed relentlessly at my heart these four times. On many sleepless nights, my pillow was a garden watered by rushing, gushing bitter tears.

"Why not go to the hospitals for such diseases are curable? You will save your children's lives which once lost are irretrievable. What parents are you? Hatching healthy chicks and always leading them to a starving snake's nest," concerned neighbours braved to say knowing very well, however, that their effort was as futile an exercise as trying to single-handedly empty the brimming sea.

My husband and I remained mum. Soon such advisers lost heart and gave up. We knew too, that any form of persistence would be tantamount to wasting rare and precious pebbles on grasshoppers when the surrounding forests teem with doves, hares and guinea-fowls.

"You claim to be prayer veterans for nothing. Where are the miracles? After all, are these the days of miracles?" some cynics shouted at us once they were out of our yard.

Naturally, we just brushed this aside as spittle or rotten broken eggs aimed at spoiling the rest in the basket. So my husband and I (the church people backing us fully) learnt to be content in our discontent. Then sleeping gales awoke. Our close relatives.

"Can't you really read riddles? Grown-ups like you! Do you take these deaths as blessings? This new faith you have tenaciously and unquestioningly clung onto ….! One day it will land you in the midst of the proverbial pit-trap so infested with lethal pointed sticks. Then you will begin to see and reason. Are you wood or stones void of feelings? After all, is Goredema not one of your church members? When he got ill, did he not go to the mission hospital, recuperated and later went back to your wretched sect? Is he not in your church today? How many of your members scud for hospitals when trouble knocks threateningly on their doors? Are they foolish and blind moles? "

Seething waters always cool, that we knew so we allowed them to fume. They always calmed and found us the same old individuals. We had proved as unshakable and as steadfast as anything could be.

In spite of the pinch I felt at the death of each child, I taught myself to dig up little graves where I hastily buried every prickly thought, feeling and even words. Even events. Anything that haunted or perturbed me. I learnt to live with hope for someone had advised me years ago. "Hope brings meaning to life. When one stops hoping one's world begins to crumble down." So I struggled to hope. At last I hoped and could feel my pensive bleeding heart healing and my cloudy sky fast clearing. I rejoiced with my husband. Ba Shamiso. Why could we not rejoice for what birds could dare brave such storms? Such gales? We had heroically sacrificed four souls. I was quite confident that one day, when called upon to sacrifice ourselves, we would gladly do so too. This, we never communicated openly with Ba Shamiso — it was tacit.

Now, Ba Shamiso ails. Our members have been here several times but there seems to be no improvement at all. We smell sure death! He continues to groan and gasp for breath rarely speaking but looking vacantly at the grass thatch. Then, today he has writhed piteously from dawn to this noon. He has rolled again and again but the showers of prayers have yielded no fruits.

"Hospital! Take me there or I die." he says at last.

"Have I heard well?

'Hospital! My stomach burns. It is hurting. Hurry with me or I ---," he clamours!

"Hospital?" I ask.

He avoids my eyes. Something inexplicable fills them up. It's something I can't name for I have not known or experienced it before. I know everything should have a name, so perhaps one day, I will come up with one. I mean coin one.

Now, I feel it clearly; a large, cold sharp sword eating cruelly into the core of my heart leaving it deeply incised and bleeding endlessly, profusely. I know that soon, naughty green flies – the sort that befriends shit-will soon buzz over my fresh gaping wounds to sow their tiny maggots so generously. Overnight, my heart will become fertile ground for such sort of thing! "How can you say that?" my lips found themselves asking.

I'll be cleansed and go back to church," the wriggling heap says looking at the unspeaking walls. My blood boils. My love and concern for him begin to melt away and drifts down rapids and falls. Hope! I frantically grope for it in its nest. This time, it's not there. It has flown away never to return to its nest. I call upon you the four little great heroes of mine. Arise and hearken such foul words. Stir in your shallow graves and hearken. Selfishness and hypocrisy at their best. Betrayer of ideals one has set for oneself and vowed to cherish. This brute, this stone, feels the heat which the tenderest could not feel and were made not to feel. Weaponed, he flees armies which his weaponless subjects advanced valiantly to confront.

How I am now forced to exhume all the little graves where I have hid the scars of my woes and wars. I'll too exhume every tinny grave of forgetfulness. Am I any different from the witch of the night? Oh, my labour pains, come and witness all this! Such razors. Such bombs. Such poison. Such thorns.

"See Ba Shamiso. You and I allowed four souls to die. Allowed starving hawks to tear them in our faces. Unflinching talons sank into their tender flesh and crooked hooks plucked chunks away. We endured all that for we had a conviction that we were totally right and committed to our ideals. How I wish you had decided otherwise before those tragedies. Wouldn't our yard be full of joyous, youthful noise? Hollering sounds of children. Wouldn't our children be herding the stubborn goats, sheep and cattle we run after in the vleis?"

He is dump and looks away eternally as my fiery darts fly at him. I bet you, just as he decided the fate of my dead children. How can one return to his vomit? Even if he wants to, I will not allow him. It's too late. He will die here like my children. On that I am stubborn as death itself. Hospital! A word that once made Ba Shamiso suffer from nausea.

*****2001****

HWINDI THE TOUT

There are basically three aspects I detest about our growth point. First, the public toilets. They are nearly always an eyesore for, every morning, they are in a real mess. If you are a stranger and you happen to disembark one of the earliest buses and rush to the toilets, you have to be wary or you will suddenly get your feet bogged down in heaps upon heaps of stinking, nauseating fresh stools right at the entrance. You still have to help yourselves anyway, for these are the only available public toilets, so you momentarily pretend not to be seeing anything, stop right at the entrance, look away, upwards at the grey walls and urinate. If you want to use squat holes, it is tough luck for you have an impassable roadblock to contend with. People allege the *hwindis* are responsible for the mess. I just don't know but anywhere, can one use the toilet responsibly when darkness reigns in there all night? All electric lights are vandalised. Although I am hesitant to take the touts as scapegoats, I must hasten to say I hate them. I mean the touts. I also hate the beer outlet—a grotesque and shoddy structure built from asbestos sheets right on the terminus ground. It is the base for the *hwindis*. They clog around it like flies on carrion. After looting people's monies, they rush there to buy scuds of opaque beer. It is the scuds for which people are harassed and tormented daily on the wretched bus terminus.

As I feared, when our old, battered and squeaking bus entered the terminus, the legion of touts swarmed towards it whistling madly and hammering its metal sides deafeningly with their calloused grubby hands. It was disgusting but what could one do? Everyone feared them. I believe even their biological parents. "They have utterly no conscience," I have heard many people say. "They are dead already and always strike fear in people," they added.

Out of the crowded bus at last, safe from the endless swirling dust and fouled air, it was with utter shock that we all learnt the touts-many of them—had invaded the bus carrier. Each was claiming a territory of luggage on the carrier. Occasionally, they growled at each other after a fierce disagreements about "border" disputes on the carrier. Anywhere, the more powerful ones always triumphed over the odds.

Startled, the passengers insulted, "Leave our luggage alone. We know you heartless stones who harass their own parents, brothers and sisters. If the conductor or loader is not available, we will bring our luggage down by ourselves." They were talking to the wind. The *hwindis* just laughed – an economic mocking laugh.

"Your hearts know very well that you are kidding. No-one will come up here. This is our territory. The bus operators know we are up here on business. Go and complain wherever you will. The police is up there at their station. Bring them here if you want," the boss, a stout young man who wore the face of an unaccomplished caretaker, pronounced.

"Come on, *VaRungu*–our good employers–show us your luggage. You will just give us a few coins as a token of appreciation for the work done," they persuaded. One man, determined to bring his luggage down by himself was brutally kicked down. Fortunately, he was not hurt. He looked appealingly at us. I was hurt. Very hurt. Everyone felt the same but appeared helpless. Rumour had it that if you beat or harass one of the touts, they would all pounce at you with the wrath of an offended god. They were like bees. Kill one of them and they will sting you to death. They had a queer sense of unity of its own kind! "Give us our luggage then but expect nothing more than mere verbal thanks. We still have long journeys ahead of us. We can't pay *hwindis*," a woman said in a shaky voice.

Soon the luggage was down. With the agility of monkeys, the touts filed down the carrier and with keen, searching eyes of an eagle, each of them hunted down his clients. The battle had begun. I watched the proceedings with keen interest. A more or less similar event was taking place between each tout and his client. "The *hwindi* needs just a scud of beer *vadhala* a few coins will do," one of the touts pronounces with feigned and exaggerated courtesy. The old man resisted. "I will report you to the police," he threatened. "There is one uniformed over that side of the terminus. I will give you a minute to go and report me. Do that old man. You think you are clever. I want a thousand dollars for my service. No less, no more," he pronounced sternly. "These people are not people anymore. They have the form of human beings but they have the heart of the beast. They are dead like wood and they have no ears. They will never hear you. Give them their due to avert kindling unnecessary fires at the rank," a bald-headed man advised.

Grudgingly but hesitantly, the affected old man handed the tout two five hundred dollar notes and walked away furiously, muttering something. Behind me, an overcharged elderly woman was pleading and crying pitifully. The young boy was persistent. He wanted his money. He got his dues and left the sorrowful woman alone. Mirthfully, triumphantly, he headed for the beer outlet and bought some scuds of opaque beer. I suppressed the urge to rush to the beer outlet and strangle him.

I was scared beyond measure. Would this happen to me or my return trip to Mataruse with my four bags of cement? I would have two wars to win; getting a ticket and loading the bags of cement. With the transport blues resulting from acute fuel shortages, who knew, I could put up at the bus terminus. I dreaded the chilly weather that characterised nights at the growth point.

Then an idea sprang up in my mind. I will hunt for a young innocent *hwindi*. I consoled myself that youth is innocence. I found one who seemed quite agreeable. He was too quick to agree with me on everything. I was a bit suspicious. Each bag of cement would be loaded onto the carrier at a cost of ZW$500-00. Four bags would be ZW$2000-00. That was a reasonable amount.

The bus came at last and I rushed to join the snaking queue. After securing a ticket and seat, I climbed down the bus and helped the young tout to load my bags. That done, I took him aside and counted the agreed money. He refused to take it. He needed ZW$1500-00 for a bag. Within seconds, all the older *hwindis* had encircled me.

"Get your money from this foolish man, sonny. He chose a young *hwindi* so that he can abuse him. He will get it thick," roared the older touts. I smelt trouble.

I remember resisting and saying a few words about being a man like any other. I would stand on our agreement with the young tout. All I remember is, I was stripped naked. All my money was gone. All over my body was a rich harvest of deep gaping wounds. The touts were boozing at the beer outlet, indifferent to my plight. A sea of eyes looked at me and pitied me. That was the furthest they could go. Sympathies. Apart from that, they were helpless.

*****2003*****

Printed in the United States
By Bookmasters